Sisters of Isis

1

The Summoning

LYNNE EWING

HYPERION/NEW YORK

For Lyla Lynne Firuza Osmanov-Fitzgerald,
who brought joy back into my life, and
also for my very patient editor, Jennifer Besser.
Thank you both.

Printed in the United States of America
First Edition
3 5 7 9 10 8 6 4 2
This book is set in 12-point Griffo Classico.
Reinforced binding
Library of Congress Cataloging-in-Publication Data on file
ISBN-13: 978-14231-0342-4
ISBN-10: 1-4231-0342-4

www.hyperionteens.com

Sleep did not fall away from Sudi at once, but in slow swings between dreams and wakefulness. She fought the dream world, struggling to come back, and when finally she rose up from deep within her mind, the sharp, cold air made her reach for her covers. She flung her hand out, searching for her quilt, and lost her balance. Her eyes flashed open, and she let out a startled cry. She was no longer in her bed, where she had gone to sleep, but outside, and falling down her front-porch steps. She grabbed the iron railing and caught herself. Her elbows and arms scraped over the twisting balusters.

She pulled herself up and stood, too frightened to do more than stare out at the grayish white clouds skittering across the moonlit sky. She couldn't remember climbing from her bed or walking down the stairs, yet she stood in front of her house, barefoot and dressed in a long, loose T-shirt that flapped wildly in the autumn wind.

The front door stood open behind her, and she could feel the heat coming from the house. Her father must have forgotten to turn the thermostat down again. Maybe she had been sleepwalking to escape the high temperature. That would explain why her nightmare had seemed so real. In the dream she had been wandering over scorching desert sand, lost among endless limestone mountains and barren valleys, her lungs barely able to take in the hot air.

But her logic didn't calm the trembling in her knees and hands. What would have happened if she had continued down to the canal or the

Potomac River and fallen into the water?

She started back inside, and as she crossed the threshold, a new worry seized her. Her parents and sisters were asleep upstairs, unaware that Sudi had left them vulnerable to predators. Sudi didn't know how long she'd been standing outside. She touched her cheek. Her skin felt cold. She hoped she hadn't let in something that didn't belong, and at the same time she didn't understand why such a concern should cross her mind. Her family lived in a safe part of the District.

As she started to close the door, a long, doleful howl made her pause. She stared out at the night, suddenly aware of another presence. She searched the shadows, sensing something staring back at her.

The cry repeated, more human than wolf, and for the briefest moment she thought someone was trying to scare her. She tried to convince herself that the wail came from a foreign breed, a diplomat's dog. After all, she lived in Washington, D.C., and unusual animals were brought here from faraway countries. Maybe this one had a peculiar bark, a feral cry.

She shut the door and slipped the deadbolt in place, then turned the thermostat down and went into the kitchen. She switched on the overhead light. If her best friend, Sara, had been there, the two of them would have been falling against each other and laughing at how frightened Sudi had become, but alone Sudi couldn't find the humor in her fear. She opened the refrigerator with tremulous fingers and pulled out a carton of cherry-vanilla ice cream.

Her cat, Patty Pie, rubbed against her leg, begging with purrs and meows for a bite. Sudi found a spoon, scooped a tad into Pie's dish, then stood over the sink and spooned a larger bite into her own mouth. She let the ice cream melt over her tongue.

As she started to dip her spoon into the carton again, Pie hissed. Sudi turned to see what had upset her cat, and as she did, she caught an image in the corner of her eye. She turned back and glanced up. Behind her reflection on the windowpane, a long, snouted face with lurid eyes and tall, pointed ears glared back at her.

The spoon fell from her hand and clanked

against the porcelain sink. Sudi stepped back, dropping the carton of ice cream. She switched off the light and stood in the dark, gazing back at the empty window frame. She wasn't sure what she had expected to see, but the wraithlike image was gone now.

She tried to convince herself that a lost dog had seen the light in the kitchen and had stood on its back paws, nose against the window, begging for her company. But such an animal would have needed to stretch to a height of seven feet at least. She didn't think that was possible.

Without considering it more, she picked up the carton of ice cream, then took a roll of paper towels and cleaned up the mess on the floor. A soft thump on the back steps near the mud porch made her freeze. She was too afraid to go and see what was making the sound.

Reason told her that it was just the stray dog, trying to get inside, but still her heart continued to pound. She didn't believe in ghosts or demons, and she had never been afraid of the night. She tried to talk herself out of her uneasiness—but then she saw Pie.

The yellow cat crouched low and backed away, appearing afraid, the fur on his back standing straight up.

Sudi's instincts took over. She raced up the stairs to her bedroom, Pie scampering beside her. The cat darted into the room ahead of her. She turned on the light, and when she closed the door, the sudden movement stirred the air and the pile of torn-up photographs on her desk fluttered before settling again.

She had spent the afternoon ripping up all of her pictures of Brian. She wanted zero reminders of him. But now she wondered if maybe the breakup with Brian was affecting her more than she wanted to admit. Brian had scared her. Did he still? Could anxiety have caused her sleepwalking?

She grabbed the masking tape from her desk drawer and tore off several pieces, then stuck them over the doorjamb and across the door. The tape wouldn't stop her from leaving her room, but she hoped that untangling it would be enough to awaken her if she did start sleepwalking again. She crawled into bed, wanting nothing more than to huddle under her covers and lose herself in dreams.

Pie jumped on the quilt, curled up beside her, and began purring noisily.

As Sudi drifted off, she thought of Brian again. They had broken up on Saturday, but the real break had come the day Dominique Dupont had transferred into Lincoln High School. Her father was the cultural attaché at the French embassy. Usually the diplomats' kids attended Entre Nous Academy, but Dominique had wanted to experience the "real" American teen life, so she had enrolled in public school.

Sudi shuddered, trying to push memories of Brian away. She should have felt grateful that they were through, so why did she keep crying? It wasn't as if she had really been crazy about Brian, anyway. She had liked Scott, but Brian had asked her out first, and by her third date with Brian, everyone was calling them a couple.

Then Brian had revealed a darker side, and everything about their relationship had changed. What had made her go back for more?

She drifted off, her mind replaying the memory of the night she wanted to forget.

* * *

Morning came before Sudi was ready. She blinked at the sunlight, grateful to find herself in bed. The masking tape still bridged the crack between her wall and the door, and the fear she had experienced the night before felt like a fading dream. She pulled the covers over her head and rolled over.

Her cheek hit something hard. Her eyes opened.

A snake lay beside her.

She jumped out of bed and choked on a scream. The reptile was made of bronze, maybe four feet long, and inlaid with blue and green stones that mimicked a viper's skin. She picked it up, surprise mingling with curiosity. It might have been someone's staff or walking stick. She smoothed her hand over the symbols etched in the sides. The tiny pictures looked like Egyptian hiero-glyphs. Her fingers caressed the beetles, frogs, and baboons.

The images squirmed beneath her touch until they were streaming down the rod.

She cried out and dropped the snake. The rod clanked on the hardwood floor.

She rubbed her hand down her T-shirt, trying

to erase the unpleasant feeling on her skin. Sunshine reflecting off the bronze had probably given the impression that the images were moving, but that didn't explain the strange throbbing beneath her fingers. She looked around wondering how the snake had gotten into her bed.

A sudden gust blew through her open window and caught the pile of torn-up photographs. Bits and pieces of Brian's face whirled around her. The sheer panels between the drapes had been pulled aside, and the window screen rested against the wall. Maybe she had gone sleepwalking again after all.

Panic-stricken, she examined her hands and knees for proof that she had crawled out onto the porch roof while still asleep. She imagined herself digging through a neighbor's trash, finding the horrible walking stick, and bringing it home.

She picked it up again and ran her fingers over the markings. The symbols remained still. She sighed and closed her window, then ripped off the masking tape and threw open her door.

The doorknob continued thumping against the wall as she ran down the hallway and into the bathroom. She locked the door, then stared at her swollen eyelids in the bathroom mirror. Everyone was going to know she had been crying. But that wasn't her biggest concern. She and Brian shared the same friends, so what happened now? Did Dominique just replace Sudi, or did they both fit into the same group?

She thought of the three girls in her drama class, loners who didn't belong. Kids made fun of them, and to avoid the taunts the girls ducked through the crowded hallways, heads down, wearing their bulky coats in spite of the furnace heat, as if they were trying to hide inside their winter clothing. Sudi worried that she would share this same fate.

After taking a shower and drying her hair, Sudi went back to her room. She slipped into a silky purple camisole, then pulled on her tightest low-slung jeans. The new stiletto pumps were going to inflict serious pain by the end of the day. She wrapped Band-Aids around her toes and wore the shoes anyway.

Normally she put on mascara, but she couldn't chance it. The forecast of tears made it too risky. She hurried to the stairs, but as she passed her sisters' room, the silence made her pause. They were never that quiet. And why hadn't they been banging on the bathroom door, telling her to hurry so they could take their showers?

Maybe Sudi had let something into the house last night after all. Slowly, she stepped back to their door and wrapped her fingers around the knob, her heart racing in anticipation of what she would find inside their bedroom.

She opened the door and gasped. "What are you doing?" she asked, even though she knew.

Nicole and Carrie sat on the bed under their lacy pink canopy, a Ouija board between them. Their fingers tapped the planchette, and the small plastic triangle shimmied beneath their touch, then streaked across the alphabet printed in a semicircle on the board and stopped on the YES.

"Mom's going to be pissed," Sudi said. Their mother had thrown away the last Ouija board, along with a tarot deck and the dried herbs that had left a lingering scent of licorice in their room.

Nicole and Carrie turned, each tucking a wisp of waist-length, white-blond hair behind her ear. They were identical twins, but Nicole's love for potato chips and chocolate had added plumpness to her cheeks, while Carrie's picky eating habits had narrowed her oval face. They no longer wore the same size, but they still had a similar unsettling way of looking at Sudi as if they could read her thoughts.

"We're doing this for you," Nicole explained.

"Don't put what you're doing on me," Sudi said. "I have enough problems."

"Precisely," Carrie answered.

"I saw the two of you burning something in the backyard," Sudi said. "I thought you were getting rid of bad test grades, but you were practicing magic again, weren't you?"

Carrie shrugged. "We were burning chicken bones to give Brian skinny legs for hurting you. We hate him for making you cry."

"That's not nice," Sudi scolded, taking on her big-sister role even though she hoped the spell worked. "Besides, I'm the one who broke up with him," she said, practicing the words she planned to say at school. "I told him we were through."

Carrie and Nicole stared at Sudi with something close to pity in their large blue eyes. They obviously didn't believe her. If Sudi couldn't convince her twelve-year-old sisters, then how was she going to convince her entire sophomore class?

"You need something to protect you," Carrie said.

Sudi laughed. "I need a charm to protect me from bad boyfriends," she answered, but as she turned to leave, a soft rasping made her look down. The planchette slid across the Ouija board and pointed to the *S*.

"How'd you do that?" Sudi asked. The board hadn't tilted, and neither of her sisters had moved.

"We didn't," Nicole said excitedly. "It's speaking to us."

Nicole and Carrie put their fingers back on the plastic pointer. The planchette slid to the *U*, then twirled back and pointed to the *D*.

"It's going to be a message for you, Sudi," Nicole whispered, as if speaking too loudly might interrupt the board's concentration.

"You know I don't believe in that kind of stuff," Sudi answered and started downstairs.

In the kitchen she grabbed an apple and bit

into it as she walked through the back porch and out into the yard. She stood under the kitchen window and examined the wet grass. She saw no paw prints in the soggy earth or nose smudges on the windowpane. Maybe she had imagined the dog after all.

When she reentered the house, Carrie and Nicole stood in the kitchen, waiting for her, their faces solemn.

"You need to know something," Carrie said.

Sudi rolled her eyes. "I don't need your Ouija board to know my life is trash."

The twins gasped.

"Don't say that," Nicole scolded. "Words have power . . ."

". . . And what you say will come true," Carrie finished. "It's a scientifically proven fact that you'll eventually become whatever you call yourself."

"Then you two had better be careful," Sudi snapped back, "because if you keep messing around with the occult, you're going to turn into little hags who marry toads and—" Sudi stopped. She was taking her anxiety out on her sisters. "Sorry," she whispered and stepped past them.

"Today could be dangerous for you," Nicole warned. "The Ouija board is always right."

"Someone is after you," Carrie added.

"And I suppose it's someone *eeeeviiiilll*," Sudi said, mockingly stretching *evil* into a sinister Halloween melody. She left the kitchen, grabbed her sweater from the hall closet, tugged it on, and turned to leave.

Her sisters stood behind her, blocking her way.

"Listen to us for once," Nicole pleaded.

Their worried expressions almost made Sudi believe that something bad *was* going to happen.

"You have to stop this," Sudi said gently. "It isn't healthy. That's why Mom threw away all that occult stuff. You need to understand that when your kindergarten teacher told you that twins have a psychic connection to each other, she didn't mean that the two of you are psychics, or that you have supernatural powers."

She kissed Nicole, then Carrie, and headed out the door.

At the corner, Sudi glanced back at the house. Her sisters stood together on the porch, their nightgowns waving in the breeze, staring after her. Sudi didn't believe in their connection to another world, but, looking at them, she wondered what message the Ouija board had given them.

CHAPTER 2

The printer whirred, pushing out paper copies of the Web site on sleepwalking. Sudi leaned back and put drops in her eyes, which were dry and red from staring at the computer screen. Then she pulled the band from her ponytail and ruffled her hair.

School had ended, but she had stayed late, searching for information on somnambulism. Stress had probably caused her sleepwalking, and for that reason she had decided not to tell her mother about the episode unless it happened again—and maybe she wouldn't even tell her then—because if she did, her mother would start questioning Sudi, searching for the cause, and Sudi didn't want anyone to know the truth. She hadn't even told Sara about that night with Brian.

Sudi grabbed the printouts and stuffed them into her backpack on top of her shoes, then left the computer room and started up the stairs, barefoot except for the grimy Band-Aids wrapped around her sore toes. The blisters on her heels burned. She'd only worn the killer shoes for Brian, but he hadn't even come to school. Sudi had learned through friends that his dad was being honored at the Pentagon, and Dominique had attended the ceremony with Brian and his family.

As she passed Brian's locker, an unwanted memory came back to her. The first time they had driven over to Virginia, Brian had steered his car down a dark street where no one could witness what they were going to do. She had thought he wanted to take their relationship further, but his mind had never been on kissing her. Instead he asked her to drive his huge old Cadillac, even though she didn't have a license.

Then Brian had put on his skates, and, knees bent like a skier, he had taken hold of the car bumper while she started the engine. She drove down the paved roads, while Brian kept yelling at her to go faster. She pressed her foot down on the gas pedal until wind snapped through the window and tousled her hair.

The oncoming lights flashed again in her mind, and she flinched. If the SUV hadn't swerved, she would have killed Brian and maybe others. But instead of being upset, Brian had said the near-crash had been his best ride ever. He was into skitching and car surfing—anything extreme.

How many times had he forced her to drive down those same roads? Why hadn't she been able to tell him no?

She should have felt relieved that Brian was going out with Dominique now, but Sudi had an uneasy feeling that her bond with Brian wasn't broken. She didn't know what she would do if he called again and she didn't understand why she had taken such risks. It was as if something dormant inside her had awakened, a part of her she had never known before, and it scared her.

By the time she reached the second-floor landing, the sun had set, leaving the corridor in dusky light. The silence made her pause. The band practiced every day after school. Normally, the off-key tones from clarinets and flutes filled the air. She glanced at her watch. It was almost seven. She couldn't have been on the computer that long without being aware of the hours slipping away.

The sound of footsteps in the stairwell broke the quiet, but knowing that someone else wandered the deserted hallways with her did not comfort her now. She tiptoed to her locker, not understanding the intense need to hide. The feeling nagged at her even though reason told her she was safe.

Maybe she should have listened to her sisters' warning after all. She looked up and down the hallway, not sure what she expected to see, before she worked her combination. She opened her locker and caught her reflection in the heart-shaped mirror on the door. Her hair was parted on the wrong side, exposing a section of the birthmark on her scalp.

As she started to fix her part, a hand clamped down on her shoulder.

Sudi tried to turn and lost her balance.

Carter grabbed her arm and steadied her. "What's wrong?" he asked.

"You startled me," she said and started to laugh, but stopped. She had looked both ways down the hallway and hadn't seen him. "Did you sneak up on me?"

"Why would I do that?" he asked with a slow, easy grin, and rested his hand on the locker above her. He edged closer and looked down at her as if he were seeing her for the first time. He tilted his head until his lips were dangerously close to kissing her.

"Carter," she said, flustered. "We're best friends."

"Just testing," he teased.

She shook her head. Girls at school warned each other to stay away from him, but they never followed their own advice. No one could resist him even with his reputation as a heart-breaker.

"Brian is an idiot," Carter said, interrupting her thoughts. "I told him so when he started going out with Dominique."

His fingers ran down her arm. She pulled away, then hesitated. Maybe he was only offering her the comfort of friendship. He squeezed her hand.

"It's pretty funny the way you ruined Dominique's boots," he went on. "Brian told me she's making him buy her a new pair."

"It was an accident," Sudi protested. "The lemonade slipped out of my hand."

"No one believes you," Carter said and shot her a wry smile.

"You know I'd tell you if I'd done it on purpose." She tried to concentrate on which books she needed to take home, but her mind jumped back to Saturday, the day she and Brian had broken up.

Sudi had bought lunch at the Bread Line, a small restaurant on Pennsylvania Avenue near the White House, and as she bit into the crusty bread and sweet Italian sausage, Brian and Dominique had walked inside, holding hands. When Brian leaned over to kiss Dominique, his gaze fell on Sudi. She immediately marched over to Brian, planning to tell him that they were through, but the drink she was holding dropped from her hand, splashing over Dominique's pricey boots. Sudi fled in embarrassment.

"Can I give Scott your cell number?" Carter asked.

"Scott?" Sudi asked, hoping she didn't sound too breathless.

"I didn't know if you were ready," Carter answered. "You look like you landed pretty hard."

"I'm through with Brian," she mumbled, not sure that she was, and reached into her locker. She pulled a folder from under her rolled-up sweater, and a stack of test papers spilled forward.

"Scott's been waiting for you to figure out that Brian's all wrong for you," Carter said, but his eyes never met hers. He stared at the lopsided pile of tests, then ran his fingers through the pages as if checking her grades. He seemed to be looking for something.

"You can give Scott my number," Sudi answered, but a thought occurred to her as she pulled her shoes from her backpack and slipped them onto her wounded feet. "How do you know Scott?"

"He plays rugby," Carter answered, and then, abruptly, he began jogging backward. "I'll catch you tomorrow," he yelled before turning and sprinting away.

Sudi glanced into her locker and wondered what Carter had expected to find. She pulled out her sweater, and a white envelope glided after it, skating across the floor. She picked it up. URGENT was written across the front. She ripped the seal, pulled out a square piece of paper and read the message.

Our meeting cannot be put off any longer. Come to the Hotel Washington, Sky Terrace restaurant, sunset. I will tell you everything.

A thrill rushed through her. The invitation had to be from Scott. Carter's odd behavior suddenly made sense; he hadn't been looking for anything, he had been sneaking the invitation into her locker.

She stuffed her sweater inside, then twirled the combination lock, grabbed her backpack, and hoped she wasn't too late.

CHAPTER 3

Sudi dropped her backpack on a love seat near the door, straightened her lacy camisole and stepped into the crowded Sky Terrace restaurant. The warm evening air wrapped around her, bringing the lush smells of frying onions and seafood. Even the night views of the White House and the Washington Monument were perfect for a first date. Her stomach fluttered in anticipation.

When Scott didn't come forward to greet her, she headed toward the end of the terrace, where people stood clustered in small groups. Maybe Scott had invited her to a gathering of Entre Nous students.

Halfway there, she noticed a young man, seated at a table near the railing, waving at her. At first, she thought he was trying to get the attention of someone behind her, but then he called her name. "Sudi!"

She swerved around a fast-moving waitress and started toward him, assuming he was a friend of Scott's. He had the Entre Nous look: a three-hundred-dollar haircut and a jacket that cost more than Sudi spent on clothing in an entire year.

"I'm Abdel," he said, rising to greet her, and took her hand. Then, motioning to a girl seated beside him, he added, "This is Meri."

Everyone in D.C. knew Senator Stark's daughter. Meri attended Entre Nous and was usually surrounded by photographers and bodyguards. Her mother had made one bid for her party's presidential nomination, and political analysts said that this year the senator would succeed.

Meri waved and looked toward the exit, as if she were about to use Sudi's arrival as an excuse to leave. Maybe Abdel had been a blind date and Meri was unhappy with the match—although on the surface, Sudi couldn't see any reason for Meri to be displeased.

"I'd also like you to meet Dalila," Abdel added.

Sudi had never seen Dalila before, and she definitely would have remembered meeting her. Dalila was breathtakingly beautiful, despite her shaven head and the strange tattoo above her right temple.

"I'm pleased to meet you," Dalila said quietly.

"Hi," Sudi answered, looking around. "Where's Scott?" She took a seat next to Abdel.

"Scott?" Abdel asked.

"Scott Johnston," Sudi said. "He asked me to meet him here."

"I asked you here," Abdel corrected her. He handed her a menu.

"You sent me the invitation?" Sudi asked, surprised.

"I needed to meet with the three of you."

Abdel set his arms on the table and leaned forward. "I've been sent to the United States by the Hour priests, a secret society—"

"Sheesh," Meri said and fell back in her chair. "Is this some weird way to meet my mother?"

"Why would I want to meet her?" Abdel asked.

"Because everyone in this town wants to speak to her," Meri answered curtly. "And FYI, you won't get a meeting with her through me. I only came here because you gave me such a valuable gift." She held up a rod with the head of a snake that looked like the one Sudi had found on her bed earlier. "My mother told me I had to return this to you."

"It's an apotropaic wand," Abdel explained. "The ancient Egyptians used it for protection. And you can't return it to me, because it belongs to you."

"That excuse is not going to work with my mom," Meri said and placed the snake on the table.

"Maybe after I explain why I've been sent here, you'll want to keep it," Abdel said. "The three of you are descended from the divine pharaohs of ancient Egypt."

Dalila nodded knowingly, suggesting that his revelation wasn't a secret to her. But Meri and Sudi just stared at each other, then burst into spontaneous laughter.

"Do I look regal?" Meri asked between giggles. She was thin and tomboyish, her hair falling into her eyes.

"Abdel is telling the truth," Dalila insisted.

"I was born in Nebraska," Sudi answered pulling on a strand of silky blond hair. Her eyes were blue, her skin pale cream. She didn't look Egyptian. "My family has lived in North America since the Dutch settled Delaware in 1631. So how can I be related to a pharaoh?"

"Because you are," Abdel answered. "And now you must stand against evil and defend the world."

"Right," Meri said and folded her arms over her chest, solemn again.

"Because we're superheroes," Sudi added sarcastically and smiled. She'd played enough pranks on other people to recognize this as someone's practical joke, but who would go to such an extreme? Then she thought of Brian and the new boots he had to buy for Dominique. But he was the one who had dumped *her*. Could he really be that upset with her?

Abdel spoke again, "Since the goddess Isis gave the Hour priests the Book of Thoth, the priests have devoted their lives to stopping the forces of darkness. So, when the Cult of Anubis turned up in Washington, D.C., we were concerned."

Everyone in D.C. had heard about the cult: a new age group from California that had opened a spa, offering relaxation and pleasure for overworked Washingtonians. But Sudi had also heard rumors about therapies that sounded more like magic than cures, and elaborate secret ceremonies performed for members only.

"The cult leaders plan to destroy the bloodline of Horus and return the universe to the chaos from which it came," Abdel said, breaking into Sudi's thoughts. "They'll use demons and—"

"Do you expect me to believe that?" Sudi asked. For a practical joke it was pretty lame, but then another idea came to her, and she suddenly wished she had worn makeup and her push-up bra because this had to be a new reality show. It made sense to her now. Dalila looked drop-dead gorgeous and was probably the hostess, and Meri was a celebrity. Sudi had an image of her sisters writing to the producers and proposing Sudi, the ultimate skeptic, for their show. She lifted her glass of water, trying not to look too obvious, and glanced around, searching for the hidden cameras and microphones.

Abdel reached into a worn leather pouch and pulled out three tattered beige scrolls with dark brown striations.

"These are papyri from the Book of Thoth," he said and handed one to each girl. "You'll need the incantations written here to fight the creatures sent to destroy you."

Sudi touched the frayed edges and unrolled the scroll, then ran her finger over the images of rabbits, snakes, and eyes.

"Only the divine heirs to the throne of Egypt have the power to use the magic in the Book of Thoth to stop the dark forces freed by the cult," Abdel explained.

"Oh, okay, sure. I'll just use my Saturday nights to protect the city from mummies," Sudi scoffed, as she imagined her friends laughing when the program aired on TV.

"You don't really believe this stuff, do you?" Meri asked Abdel. "It's bunk."

Abdel scowled. "You must believe me. The cult leaders could be contacting you already, using a spell to make you walk to them while you're still asleep."

A chill swept through Sudi. How could the show's producers know about her sleepwalking? It had to be just a coincidence. Or maybe Carter was in on it and he had seen what she had been researching in the computer room.

"You're wasting my time," Meri said tiredly and glanced at the other end of the terrace, trying to get someone's attention. "I need to go home and study."

"I'm telling you the truth," Abdel said, his voice rising. "And the proof is in the identical birthmarks you each have beneath your hair."

Sudi reached up and touched her head, then looked across the table. Meri had done the same. They both glimpsed the eye on Dalila's scalp, then looked back at each other again.

"Your birthmarks look like the one that Dalila has above her temple," Abdel explained. "It's the sacred eye of Horus."

"I've heard enough," Meri said.

Abdel turned to Dalila. "Help me convince them that I'm telling the truth."

"Why should I, when no one told me the truth?" Dalila asked, her large eyes becoming glassy with tears.

"Your uncle said that he had reared you to be the perfect heir." Abdel seemed truly shocked.

"The heir to some fortune, I thought. I assumed I was being groomed to marry some rich prince from Saudi Arabia," she replied.

"You were taught the old ways," he argued.

"So I would be a treasure to my people when I married and moved to the Middle East," Dalila shot back.

Sudi watched Dalila. She was definitely over-playing for the cameras.

"No one ever told me I had to fight demons. And, although I don't understand your reasons for doing so, I know you're lying." Dalila grabbed a shawl from the back of her chair, flung it around her like an actress leaving the stage, and stormed off.

"That's it," Meri said, picking up her scroll.

"And, Abdel, take me off your invite list, because I'm definitely not coming to another one of your dinners, no matter how much my mother insists that I should."

Abdel clasped her wrist.

"Let go of me," Meri yelled and tried to yank her hand back, but his hold was powerful.

At the other end of the terrace two men got up from their chairs. One had taken off his jacket, and his husky chest and arms barely fit into his short-sleeved shirt. The other, taller than the first, had a hard, sunburned face. He flung his chair out of the way and marched forward, bumping into the table edges.

"Let go of her!" he shouted with booming authority.

Diners and waiters became silent. The thump-thumping of the two presidential helicopters landing on the White House lawn were the only sounds on the terrace.

"You must listen to me," Abdel pleaded, holding Meri's arm. "Your life is in danger. Do you think the cult leaders will let you live?"

"Look behind you," Meri challenged.

Abdel glanced over his shoulder. The two men had pulled guns, and their attention was focused intently on Abdel.

Diners screamed, and a table toppled over as people stampeded toward the exits.

But instead of releasing Meri, Abdel grabbed her head.

Meri cursed and flung her arms, pounding on his back.

Sudi froze, undecided. This wasn't like any reality show she'd ever seen before; Meri looked truly distressed. Maybe Abdel was just a rich guy living in his own fantasy world.

Sudi clutched Abdel's arm, trying to help Meri. She dug her fingernails into his skin, but Abdel didn't flinch.

"Release her," the taller man yelled again.

Abdel ignored the order and spread his fingers in Meri's hair, then bowed his head until it rested against her forehead. He spoke in a language that Sudi didn't understand and had never heard before.

Meri stopped struggling and tilted her head, looking into Abdel's eyes, transfixed.

The two men with the guns lunged forward. The taller one grabbed Sudi around the waist and pulled her out of the way. Then both men wrestled with Abdel, trying to rescue Meri, but Abdel didn't let go until he had finished speaking.

When he released her, she collapsed into the burly man's arms. The taller one slipped his gun back into its holster and tried to handcuff Abdel, but Abdel shoved him aside and turned to Sudi.

Sudi had no idea what Abdel wanted with her, but she no longer believed this was a practical joke, or a new reality show. She eased backward, afraid, and bumped into a table, knocking over a glass. Water trickled onto the floor near her feet.

Still clutching the scroll, she spun around and tried to run. Her feet slipped on the ice cubes and water. She almost fell, then regained her balance and dashed into the hallway. She grabbed her backpack, kicked out of her shoes, and sprinted down the carpet.

A gun fired as she ran for the elevator.

"Come on. Come on." She furiously hit the call button.

Abdel stepped out of the restaurant and ran toward Sudi as the metal doors opened. She rushed inside and pushed LOBBY, then DOOR CLOSE.

She fell back against the wall, gasping for air.

An arm shot between the closing doors, and Abdel slipped inside. The doors shut behind him, and the elevator started down.

Sudi tried to punch the alarm button, but Abdel grabbed her hand and kissed the tips of her fingers.

"Please," Sudi said. "Don't touch me."

"Don't be afraid," he whispered and clasped her head in his hands, pulling her toward him.

Sudi whimpered.

Abdel rested his lips against her forehead, his breath warm on her face, and spoke the same strange language he had spoken to Meri.

"Heb menekh hekau," he whispered. *"Uab ab-ek. Hu en na ek nifu er fet-ef."*

And then, unexpectedly, Sudi understood the words. Or was it that he was speaking English again? She wasn't sure. Her nerves were raw, and her heartbeat thundered in her ears.

"Sublime of magic," Abdel continued. "Your

heart is pure. To you I send the power of the ages."

In spite of being in a closed elevator, wind blew into Sudi's nostrils and filled her lungs. Her chest heaved, trying to catch a breath not tainted with the smell of tombs.

Abdel forced her head down, and then his lips moved against her hair, over her birthmark.

"Divine one," he whispered. "Come into being. I awaken the soul of ancient Egypt, lying dormant in your soul."

He released her.

Her knees buckled, and he caught her before she fell.

When the elevator doors opened, Sudi grabbed her backpack and scrambled out into the reception area. She collided with Meri's bodyguards, who had run down the stairs.

As the elevator closed, the two men forced the doors open and looked inside.

The elevator was empty.

"Where did he go?" the taller one shouted at Sudi.

Sudi shook her head. "I didn't see."

"Wait here," he commanded.

But pure instinct was driving Sudi now. She needed to go someplace safe, and that meant home.

When the men ran off, Sudi hurried outside.

Sirens filled the night. Secret Service agents climbed from black sedans and charged inside.

Still in a daze, Sudi ran across Fifteenth Street and headed north, crossing into Lafayette Park in front of the White House. She slouched on a bench in the darkness, her knees shaking too violently to continue.

Her scalp itched, and her birthmark burned. She opened her backpack, searching for her mirror. The tattered scroll was resting on top even though she couldn't remember putting it there. She started to throw it away, then thought better of it, crushed it under her books, and found her mirror. She studied herself, wondering what Abdel had done to her. Wisps of hair stood in a halo around her head as though she had walked through a cloud of static electricity.

"Sudi?" Someone called her name.

She jumped up, ready to run, her bare feet stinging with blisters and cuts.

Scott walked toward her in a slow, even stride. He still wore his school uniform: gray slacks, blue blazer, and white shirt. He had loosened his red tie. His curly brown hair brushed against his collar, and in the dim light he looked more handsome than her memory of him. He still had his California tan even though he lived in D.C. with his grandmother now. Rumor had it that he had gotten into trouble with drugs back in Los Angeles.

"What's wrong?" he asked with true concern in his voice.

"Just a bad case of the frizzies," she answered, trying to sound lighthearted when all she wanted was to fall into his arms and cry. Her day could not possibly get worse—and then she saw Michelle.

Michelle strutted toward them. The Entre Nous uniform jacket fit most girls like a box, but Michelle had had hers tailored to accentuate every curve. The top two buttons of her white shirt were undone, offering a view of her lace bra and cleavage.

"Hey, Sudi," Michelle said and wrapped her hands possessively around Scott's arm. Sudi and Michelle had been best friends through elementary school, but in junior high Michelle had been accepted into the academy, and the two of them had quickly grown apart.

But instead of responding to Michelle's challenge, Sudi walked away, her brain too flustered and confused to let her engage in flirtatious combat over Scott.

"Sudi," Michelle called after her, sounding disappointed.

"Later," Sudi replied over her shoulder.

"Do you need a ride?" Scott yelled.

She shook her head in response and continued to the street. At the curb, she hailed a cab and eased inside. She waved good-bye and closed her eyes, grateful no one would be home yet. On Monday nights her sisters had dance lessons, and her mom and dad always took them out to eat afterward.

A short ride later, Sudi hurried inside her house and ran upstairs to her parents' bedroom. She opened the chest at the foot of their bed. The smell of cedarwood filled the air. She pulled out her baby-photo album and fanned through the pages.

In every picture, a bonnet or cap or blanket covered her head. And then she found one. She tore it out, certain now that the eye on Dalila's scalp had been a tattoo. In the picture, Sudi's birthmark looked like an ordinary dark mole.

She sat on the edge of her parents' bed and considered what had happened. Maybe Abdel, Dalila, and Meri had only been part of some strange initiation that Sudi had to go through before she could date a guy at Entre Nous. The students were known for being snooty and sticking together, excluding outsiders. She imagined Abdel telling Scott everything that Sudi had done. Maybe they had even videotaped it and were watching her now, laughing at the fear in her eyes.

Sudi tossed the photo back into the chest and slammed the lid back down. No guy was worth that kind of trouble, not even a hottie like Scott.

CHAPTER 4

Sudi crunched into the dill pickle she was sharing with Sara, then took a sip of Coke and handed both back to her friend. She had thought the class trip to the Smithsonian Institute would be an easy way to avoid Brian and Dominique, but when she stepped onto the school bus that morning, she had found herself face to face with the two of them, embraced in a kiss.

She had tossed them a friendly smile, even

though she had wanted to spit. But what she remembered most was the way Dominique had smelled of jasmine and roses. The designer perfume was something Sudi's mother would never have bought for her.

"How can Dominique look so beautiful at the end of the day?" Sudi complained. Dominique was walking by herself toward the line of school buses parked in front of the Washington Monument.

Sara turned, her rhinestone skull earrings jangling against her necklaces.

"Dominique is wondering the same about you," Sara said. "I bet she rubs her skin raw trying to get the glow that comes naturally to you. And her curly bun is definitely an add-on." Sara grabbed a fistful of Sudi's blond tangles. "No one can compete with this. Your hair is gorgeous, and so are you."

"You're the best friend ever," Sudi said and hugged Sara.

"Aw, quit with the mushy stuff." Sara tossed the remains of the pickle and Coke into a trash bin. "Where do you want to go next?"

Sudi glanced at her watch. "It's time to go back to the bus."

"We can't leave without visiting Minister Cox," Sara said and pulled on Sudi's arm. They dodged the oncoming joggers and hurried across the treelined lawn to the National Museum of Natural History.

At the security station, Sudi unzipped her backpack. The guard stuck a wooden stick inside and shone the beam of a flashlight around the grinning monkey faces on her Paul Frank pajamas. She was spending the night with Sara so they could finish their class project on space travel.

After Sara passed through the security check, the two of them ran around the African elephant display in the center of the rotunda, took the escalator down to the ground floor, and rode the elevator near the Constitution Avenue entrance up to the Origins of Western Culture exhibit on the second floor.

"I love all the cubbies and alcoves in this exhibit," Sara said, rushing around the diorama of an early man drawing a bison on a cave wall. "This would be the best place in the world for a game of hide-and-seek."

They stopped in front of the outer coffin of

Tenet-Khonsu, an ancient Egyptian high priestess.

Sudi had told Sara everything that had happened the night before with Abdel. Now Sara looked at the hieroglyphs. "Tell me what they say."

Sudi had seen the same pictographs before, but this time she felt she could decipher their meaning. She read out loud, *"I have not sullied the world of the Nile. . . ."*

She stopped. How could she know what the symbols meant? Yet she was confident that she had interpreted them correctly.

"Show-off," Sara teased and playfully elbowed her. "Did Abdel teach you how to read hieroglyphs, too?"

"Lucky guess," Sudi answered. She couldn't, of course, read in any language except English. Yet somehow she knew the meaning of the symbols inscribed on the coffin.

"But it's a cool idea," Sara said with a scampish grin. "We could bring Abdel and Dalila here, and you could pretend like you can read the hieroglyphs, and you could tell them something dire." Sara started laughing, her imagination taking hold of her.

Sudi gave her a look. "I don't want to continue the game with Abdel and Dalila. I just want to forget it ever happened."

"You will," Sara said and moved on to the mummy called Minister Cox. She tapped the glass. "Can you imagine having your bones on display in a museum? They should make it against the law."

Sara talked as she always did about the unfairness of denying Minister Cox a proper burial, but Sudi walked on to the next coffin and concentrated on the hieroglyphs. She understood the text. How was that possible?

Finally, she read the inscription out loud. *"As for anyone who might pass, pause and make an offering, that I might be well remembered—"*

"Stop," Sara said and nudged her. "You're creeping me out now. You made the words sound too real."

Sudi clenched the strap on her backpack, trying to stop a sudden sense of falling. If she could read the ancient writing, then was it possible that the other things Abdel had told her were also true? She took a quick step back and caught herself.

"What's wrong?" Sara asked.

Sudi shook her head. "Nothing," she answered. "Have you ever heard of someone called Horus?"

"The Egyptian god Hor?" Sara asked and didn't wait for a reply. "The Greeks called him Horus. He battled the god Seth. It was that typical fight between good and evil. Horus stood for order, and Seth wanted to destroy the world. Did Abdel talk about him?"

Sudi couldn't answer, because a sudden feeling of nausea had overcome her. She rushed to the restroom at the back of the exhibit, hurried inside, and turned on the cold water, splashing it onto her face. She took several deep breaths, her head in the sink, then looked up and stared at her reflection in the mirror.

Sara appeared behind her, watching her.

"Hey, are you okay?" Sara asked.

Sudi nodded, even though her legs felt wobbly. "I think I'm coming down with the flu," she lied. She had no intention of leaving the museum until she had had a chance to study the hieroglyphs alone and find a rational explanation for what was happening. "Go on without me. I'll catch a cab."

"You know you aren't allowed to do that," Sara said.

"Do you think Mrs. Grumm wants me puking on the bus?"

"Yeah, I guess you'd start a real vomit fest," Sara laughed. She stepped closer and rubbed Sudi's back. "I'll stay with you."

"Go on," Sudi said. "I'll be okay."

"Are you sure?" Sara asked, looking doubtful.

"Please," Sudi answered and rushed into a stall pretending that she was going to be ill. "I don't want you to watch me." She slammed the door and made gagging noises until she heard Sara's retreating footsteps on the tiled floor.

Sudi waited, the leaking faucet counting out the seconds. Then she went back to the glass-enclosed display and stared at the inscriptions. She was definitely reading the hieroglyphs, or at least, in her mind she had been tricked into believing that she could. Abdel must have hypnotized her, given her a posthypnotic instruction to make her believe she could read the ancient writing even though she couldn't.

She imagined the students at Entre Nous laughing at what Abdel had done to her. Even so, she couldn't understand why she had been singled out.

A muffled noise made Sudi aware that someone was nearby. She spun around, and, when she didn't see anyone, she called out, "Hello."

Silence answered her. Something in the quiet made her tense. She sensed someone moving stealthily about.

The exhibit had alcoves, niches, and spaces under the displays where a person could hide, and hide again. But she didn't go looking for the prowler. Her mother had told her to trust her intuition, especially when she felt unsafe, so, without hesitation, Sudi made her way to the elevator.

When she was halfway there, she noticed splotches of mud on the carpet. She followed the trail to a long mound packed against the bottom of the elevator. More clay had been plastered over the frame and door.

Large oval seals were stamped on the surface, and inside each was her name, written in hieroglyphs. A panicked feeling came over her. She had listened to the short documentaries about Egyptian burial customs that ran continuously on the small screen in the museum theater and knew that seals like these had often been placed on tombs.

Someone was going out of his way to frighten her. Entre Nous students had a reputation for having an eccentric sense of humor, but she didn't think they would go this far. Maybe it was someone who had a darker side.

The lights went out, and then she knew.

"Brian," she said angrily. "This is so not funny."

When no one answered, she headed toward the gem exhibit, where the Hope Diamond was displayed, and stopped, puzzled. A wall stretched in front of the hallway that led back to the rotunda. She hadn't noticed it there before. Maybe she had just been so busy talking to Sara that she hadn't seen it.

She hurried toward the exit at the other side of the exhibit, determined not to break into a run and show fear.

But the night lighting shone unsteadily. Darkness waned and pulsed around her. She tried to focus on what was straight ahead, but the mannequins looked more real when half hidden in shadow, and she felt scared. She had an eerie sense that one of them might step from its display and start chasing her.

Finally, she saw the green exit sign and quickened her pace till she got to the bank of elevators. She pressed her finger on the call button, but the light didn't come on.

Still in near darkness, she tried the emergency exit, across from the men's restroom. She slammed against the handlebar.

The door wouldn't open. She stepped back. Locking an emergency exit was definitely against the law. But she wasn't concerned about the legality; she only wanted out. She hated the gloomy cast of shadows that seemed to move and shift around her. She pulled her cell phone from her backpack, flipped it open, and pressed her thumb on the first key, to speed-dial Sara.

Her battery was dead.

She dropped the phone back into the bag, where it landed on top of her pajamas, and realized then that when she didn't arrive home that night, no one was going to start looking for her, because her parents thought she was spending the night with Sara.

She hurried to the other end of the hallway to a door marked STAFF ONLY. She knocked and waited, hoping someone would answer and help her.

The Smithsonian museums were huge, she reasoned and, with so many visitors, people were probably locked inside all the time. If she just waited, a security guard would come through, searching for stragglers. Besides, the place was probably equipped with hidden cameras, motion detectors, and other surveillance devices. If she was patient, someone would find her.

She rummaged around in the bottom of her bag and found a half-eaten candy bar. She bit into the chocolate and walked back to the emergency exit, sat on the floor, and leaned against the wall, listening for the sound of footsteps.

Slowly, the smell of wet earth crept into her awareness. She crawled over to the door and ran her hand along the bottom, over a wet, sticky mound. Clay had been plastered around the door to seal her inside.

Reason told her that no one could take over such a public place to play a game, no matter how powerful or rich their parents might be. So what did that leave? Abdel had told her that cult leaders wanted to destroy the bloodline of Horus. Dark thoughts came to her. Maybe she was their first sacrifice. She imagined CNN broadcasting the gruesome details about her murder inside the Smithsonian.

Fear and panic overcame her rational thoughts, and terror took hold. She needed to find a place to hide. She ran back into the exhibit and crawled into the cubby under the display of Greek vases.

But as time passed and nothing happened, she began to relax. She tried to convince herself that she had no reason to be afraid. No one had ever died from being locked inside a museum overnight.

Finally, near midnight, exhausted from being vigilant, she curled up into a ball and, using her backpack for a pillow, drifted off.

Hours later, a sound roused her from her sleep. At first she didn't know where she was. Then she remembered and glanced at her watch. It read five o'clock.

Footsteps came from the other end of the hallway. She scrambled from her hiding place.

"Hello," she yelled, certain a security guard or

some member of the morning maintenance crew was close by.

She threw her backpack over her shoulder and staggered forward, trying to find whoever it was.

At the next turn, she stopped and listened again.

When she didn't hear anything, she called out, "I'm locked in. Can you help me?"

She waited. Then a soft *thud-thud-thud* came from behind her. Even as she tried to find a rational explanation for the sound, a deeper and more primitive part of her awakened and took control. Someone was trying to frighten her. She didn't believe in ghosts, but human predators did exist.

Without making a sound, she slid around the corner and hid in a dark recess, waiting, the huntress now. When the person passed in front of her, she would see who had been stalking her, without being seen. That knowledge gave her power.

She took another step to the rear of the alcove and bumped into something. She turned around and gazed into the pale blue eyes staring back at her.

CHAPTER 5

Sudi started to run, then realized she was staring at her own reflection in the glass of a darkened display case. She poked her nose closer, feeling foolish. Her heart was still pounding, and fear had left her mouth dry. She wondered vaguely if the odd taste on her tongue was the residue of too much adrenaline.

Her breath fogged the glass, and as she started to write her initials in the steam, an eerie shadow skimmed over her. The air rustled as a woman formed, her hazy image floating in the glass. She wore a helmet, or maybe the headdress was a crown. A golden vulture's head, entwined with that of a hooded cobra, jutted from the front of the headband. The woman had thick black hair and large wings.

Sudi closed her tired eyes, willing the image to vanish, but when she opened them again, the woman was still there, smiling at Sudi with a kind and loving gaze. Her wings fluttered, and the resulting breeze ruffled Sudi's hair.

"Go away," Sudi ordered. This had to be a dream, and moments from now she would awaken and—

"Why is it so hard for you to believe?" the phantom asked.

Sudi wheeled around and faced her hallucination. She took a tentative step forward, then another, and stretched out her hand until her fingertips pressed into warm, soft flesh.

"Listen well, my sister," the woman said softly. "I looked into my scrying bowl and saw that you will need the story I am going to tell."

Sudi nodded and blinked, then pinched herself, trying to wake up.

"Re-Atum emerged from the primeval ocean," the woman began, "and took the form of a Bennu-bird. Then he flew from the darkness and perched on a rock. When he opened his beak, his cry broke the silence, and with that scream he created what is and what is not to be."

"And how am I supposed to use this story?" Sudi challenged, not expecting the phantom to answer her.

"As you are dying, you will know," the woman said. "But still, you must take care when you speak the terrible words of power."

Sudi nodded and leaned back against the wall, closing her eyes. She just wanted the dream to go away.

"It's safe for you to leave the museum now," the woman said.

Sudi opened her eyes again.

The woman was gone.

Sudi had never been so relieved to have a dream end. She grabbed her backpack and ran toward the elevator.

The clay that had been packed against the metal door the night before was gone. She hurriedly pressed the call button, anxious to get out and tell Sara everything that had happened. But as she stepped inside the elevator, she looked at her hands. Her fingernails were filled with dirt.

She didn't know what Abdel had done to her, but she was determined to prove to herself that the strange things that had been happening to her had nothing to do with magic or ancient forces. As soon as she was safely back in her bedroom, she knew exactly what she was going to do.

CHAPTER 6

Sudi stepped inside her living room and breathed in the aroma of her parents' morning coffee. She listened as she closed the door behind her. Her parents always watched CNN until they left for work. The silence told her that she had the house to herself until her sisters woke up. She hurried up the stairs to her room, sat on the edge of her bed, and pulled the papyrus from her backpack.

She studied the document looking for the right incantation. She still didn't accept that she was actually reading the symbols; her mind had only been tricked into believing that she could. Even so, she picked a spell—or what she thought was one—for transforming into the Bennubird.

"Amun-Re, eldest of the gods in the eastern sky, mysterious power of wind . . ." She paused, surprised by the thin quiver in her voice. She cleared her throat and went on. *"Make a path for me to change my earthly* khat *into that of beloved Bennu.* Xu kua. *I am glorious.* User kua. *I am mighty.* Neteri kua. *I am strong."*

A long minute passed.

Nothing happened.

She grinned, satisfied that she had proven Abdel was a good hypnotist and nothing more. She wondered how long posthypnotic suggestions lasted. She'd google it and get the information after she took her shower. Grabbing clean undies and the ugly green bra her mother had bought on sale, she hurried to the bathroom and claimed it before her sisters woke up. She stripped and climbed under the hot shower spray.

The warm water took away the soreness from sleeping on the museum floor, and as the aches and pains lessened, so did the memory of the night before. She repeated the incantation, making it her own personal rap, a reminder to herself to never let her mind get carried away with fantasy again. She liked the sound the words made and repeated the spell a third time.

"Amun-Re," she said as she shaved her legs, "eldest of the gods in the eastern sky."

She soaped her arms and used her pouf as she continued, "Mysterious power of wind, make a path for me to change my earthly *khat* into that of beloved Bennu."

"*Xu kua*," she picked up the beat and stuck her face in the water. "I am glorious."

"*User kua*. I am mighty."

"*Neteri kua*. I am strong."

A pounding on the bathroom door made Sudi start. She turned off the water.

"We know you're glorious," Carrie yelled from the hallway.

"Yes, but other people have to use the shower,

O mighty one," Nicole screamed. "How long are you going to take?"

"Out in a sec," Sudi yelled back and stepped from the tub. She wrapped a towel around her and began drying off.

A sudden sharp pain in her shoulder, however, made her wince. "Ouch." She rubbed the muscle, trying to work out the pain. Tiny bumps sprouted on her skin. She didn't need a break-out, not while the weather was still warm and she could wear her halter tops.

She wiped the steam from the mirror and turned to look at her back. Hundreds of red welts spotted her skin. Just her luck. She was probably allergic to something in the museum.

She slipped into her panties and felt a feverish ache in her hip bones. Maybe she was coming down with the flu.

As she hooked her bra, downy feathers floated to the floor. She glanced up at the ceiling, but she saw nothing to explain the feathers encircling her feet.

Then, with a jab of adrenaline, she remembered the incantation she had been reciting.

"Three," she said in a shaky voice and stared back into the mirror. Didn't three times have some kind of magical power? People always said the third time's the charm.

"No," she screamed as plumage sprouted from her shoulders, neck, and ears. Her lips grew into a daggerlike beak. She opened the bathroom door as her fingers vanished. Long, slender feathers brushed over the brass knob.

She tried to call for her sisters, but a strange bird cry came out instead. *"Awk!"*

Her vision started changing. Her eyes moved to either side of her head, and each saw separately. She slammed into the wall, disoriented. She had studied the monocular vision of birds in biology, but this didn't make sense—she couldn't be turning into a bird. Things like that just didn't happen.

She pulled herself up and took one step, then swayed drunkenly as she adjusted to her new body. She tipped off the carpet runner, and her toenails scratched the wood floor. She glanced down. Short, blunt claws had replaced her feet. She stumbled and reached out to balance herself. But instead of arms, wings flapped frantically around her.

"No," she yelled in an angry tweet and hopped down the hallway to the full-length antique mirror. The reflection of a red-and-gold bird with a two-feathered crest stared back at her. She had long legs and an *S*-shaped neck.

Then she glanced outside, and for one exhilarating moment she forgot her panic, as she stared at a fanfare of colors that she had never seen before. With her bird vision she was able to see ultraviolet rays.

But her euphoria quickly faded. How was she going to change back into a girl?

She ran to her sisters' room, clucking wildly. The twins studied the occult and magic. They even tried to cast spells. Maybe they could save her.

"Nicole! Carrie!" she shouted, but their names came out as sharp, repeated tweets.

She stood in their doorway flapping her wings and shrieking, "Help me!" but only a hysterical chirping noise escaped her beak.

"A bird's trapped inside," Carrie said and grabbed a magazine. She swept it toward Sudi. "Help me shoo it out," she pleaded with Nicole.

"No," Sudi chirped, and somersaulted backward, becoming even more disoriented than before.

Carrie swung again. The magazine breezed past Sudi. She squawked and ran, spreading her wings for balance as Carrie and Nicole chased her down the stairs. Sudi tripped and rolled down the bottom three steps.

"Open the door," Carrie shouted.

Nicole sprang past Sudi. Her foot landed on the tip of Sudi's wing, pressing on the feathers.

"Okay," Nicole yelled. She flung open the front door.

Sudi jumped outside and stared back at the twins dazedly.

"Fly away," Carrie said.

Then Nicole slammed the door. The wood tapped the end of Sudi's long beak.

"Some psychics the two of you turned out to be," Sudi trilled in an angry arpeggio of peeps. "You don't even recognize your own sister."

She perched on the step and tried to hold on to the belief that this was impossible; it had to be a dream or a stress-induced hallucination. At the same time a scary idea came to her. Maybe she'd remain this way until she died. And if that happened, how was she going to convince anyone that she was a girl?

She should have learned the incantation for transforming back before she pronounced the spell to become a bird in the first place. Her chest deflated, and she squawked sadly.

She thought of her parents and felt even sadder. Would they think she had run away?

Suddenly her body tensed, and her avian instincts tore her away from her thoughts. She sensed a predator and cocked her head.

Pie was crouching toward her, back taut, ready to spring.

Sudi screeched and fluttered her wings. She rose, then fell, only to rise again before crashing back on the sidewalk and hitting her beak on the cement with a loud click. She got up again, determined not to die as a meal for her cat, and ran awkwardly, flailing her wings up and down, down and up. The motion took tremendous energy.

Pie pounced.

Sudi yelped and slipped from his claws, and then, amazingly, she took to the sky. She was airborne but afraid to stop flapping. She couldn't remember if birds continuously waved their wings. She was positive she had watched sparrows glide, but she was too afraid to stop pumping.

On the ground, Pie skulked after her, stalking his easy prey.

Wind rushed around Sudi and took her higher. She skimmed over the treetops, tearing red and yellow leaves from the branches. Then a raucous cry made her look up. A fleet of black birds dived toward her. Glossy feathers were everywhere, smacking against her. She must have flown into their territory.

She reeled, tumbling down, and hit a tree limb. Balancing herself, she perched gracelessly, leaning against the trunk. Her wings ached, her body throbbed, and she felt incredibly hungry. She snapped her beak around a beetle and swallowed it whole before she even had time to stop herself. She felt the bug squirming inside of her. Disgusted, she started to regurgitate it, but a stealthy movement made her glance down. She twisted her head and saw a swatch of yellow-orange cat climbing toward her.

Pie was unrelenting. Sudi made a mental note to feed him more cat food if she survived. He leaped. She jumped and fell from the tree, plummeting down and frantically flapping her wings.

This time the air sucked her up. She spread her feathers and glided upward on the breeze. She soared around the Washington Monument and fought the urge to dive for fish in the Potomac River.

She wondered if strange things were happening to Meri and Dalila. She swooped down and flew over traffic, following the streets to Entre Nous Academy. She didn't know how she would find Meri once she arrived, but she had to try.

Students were gathered outside the three-story red-brick building, waiting for the school day to begin.

A tall guy pointed up at her. "Look at that bird," he shouted.

"What kind is it?" another boy asked.

Sudi couldn't land with everyone watching her. What would happen if she changed back into a girl? She turned and dived into the narrow alleyway between the school and an office building.

The wind currents changed. Alarm rose inside Sudi. Her concentration flagged, and she dropped straight down, landing hard on the concrete.

She sat up and moaned—a completely human sound. The fall had made her transform back into a girl. In spite of the pain, she stood up and limped toward a line of Dumpsters.

No way she could let anyone see her like this, barefoot and naked except for her undies and the pathetically ugly green bra. She glanced up at the rows of windows in the office building and figured that a dozen or more workers had already seen her. She had no other choice—she opened the lid of a blue Dumpster, stood on a crate, and climbed inside. Settling down in the dark, holding her nose against the putrid smell, she wondered how she was ever going to explain this to her mother.

Pounding footsteps and excited voices caught her attention.

"I know the bird came down here," a voice said, from outside the metal container.

"Maybe it caught itself and kept on flying," someone answered.

Sudi winced. Was that Scott's voice? She cringed, sure that it was.

"It must be here," a girl's voice answered, sounding unquestionably like Michelle's.

Someone started to lift the Dumpster lid. Sudi slid under newspapers and flattened cardboard boxes, but there wasn't enough trash to hide her, and no way was she going to crawl beneath the slippery garbage at the bottom. She stared up at the widening crack between the container and its cover.

CHAPTER 7

"The bird's not going to be hiding in the Dumpster," Scott said. "How could it lift the lid and climb inside?"

The hinged cover fell shut again with a heavy clang of metal.

Sudi sighed and waited in the dark, breathing the stench of spoiled oranges and rotten banana peels. A rustle from something skulking over the trash made her recoil; an animal was in the bin with her. She imagined a rat nibbling on her toes and sat up, wrapping her arms around her legs and hugging her knees against her chest.

When the school bell rang, she stood and timidly lifted the heavy lid, eager to climb out, but first she peeked up at the windows in the office buildings. She had expected to see workers gathered behind the glass, watching intently to see what she would do next, but no one was staring down at her.

She threw back the cover. It banged against the wall with an angry rumble. She pulled herself up onto the lip of the metal box, and then eased out onto the crate.

Tears of frustration burned in her eyes as she carefully stepped to the ground. How was she going to get home? Maybe the best thing to do was to face the problem head on: wrap a newspaper around her waist and walk into the main office, lie and claim she didn't know what had happened to her. She imagined herself on the nightly news—a strange case of amnesia; her mother's panicked face staring into the camera, explaining to the viewing audience that Sudi had always been a nice girl. She pictured herself standing in her undies while being interviewed and all the guys at school laughing at her hideous green bra. She should have trashed it weeks ago.

Without warning a cat bolted from the Dumpster, startling her. It scampered away, then turned around and came back, meowing at her and rubbing against her ankle. Sudi leaned over and scratched behind its ears, glad that her companion had been a cat and not some long-nosed rat.

"I wish you were a dog," she whispered. "Then I could send you to find help for me."

The cat hissed at her and flicked a paw, the hairs on its back standing up in anger as if it had taken offense at her comment about the dog, and then abruptly it scuttled away.

Sudi picked a copy of *The Washington Post* out of the bin, unfolded it, and used it as a towel to cover herself.

As she started around the corner, the cat with the surly attitude returned, racing toward her. Meri followed after it, furtively glancing around as if she weren't supposed to be there. She saw Sudi and gasped.

They stared at each other, the cat circling between them.

The white highlighter didn't hide the blue-gray circles under Meri's bloodshot eyes, but far worse was the edgy fear that gripped her features. She looked like the victim of some horrible catastrophe who had been found wandering aimlessly around a destroyed neighborhood, not believing the devastation.

"Are you all right?" Sudi asked at last.

"What about you?" Meri answered. "You were that bird, weren't you?"

"No," Sudi lied.

"The cat told me you needed help," Meri said and broke eye contact. Still not looking at Sudi, she added, "and that's not the strangest thing that's happened to me since Abdel did whatever he did."

"Do you think he gave us some kind of posthypnotic suggestion?" Sudi asked.

"I thought of that," Meri replied. "Until a few seconds ago."

"What happened then?" Sudi asked.

"I wasn't the only one who saw an exotic bird fly over our school and fall from the sky," Meri challenged. "I don't think Abdel could have infected all the kids in the school yard with some kind of group hysteria."

"He doesn't go to your school?" Sudi asked, struggling to hold on to the thinnest hope that he did, and that he had been able to hypnotize the student body, like a teenage Svengali.

Meri shook her head.

In spite of the warm morning air, Sudi began to shiver. "Can you get me something to wear?"

"Wait here," Meri ordered.

Sudi edged back against the wall and wondered why she didn't have the courage to tell Meri everything. But she couldn't tell her what had happened when she didn't believe it yet herself.

Moments later, Meri returned, carrying a faded pair of jeans and an oversize purple sweater. The sneakers clutched in her hands looked as if they had belonged to a boy who climbed trees and ran through mud.

"I stole these from the clothes we're collecting for our charity drive," Meri said and sat down on the crate, watching Sudi. "I hope the shoes fit. They were the best I could find."

"Thanks," Sudi answered and glanced behind

Meri, expecting her bodyguards to round the corner.

"Where are your guards?" Sudi asked.

"Gone," Meri answered. "When weird things started happening, I knew I couldn't have those two following me everywhere. They were like barnacles."

"How'd you convince your mom?" Sudi said, letting the newspaper fall to the ground. Gray newsprint covered her thighs, and she didn't even want to consider what the black smudges were across her stomach. She tugged on the jeans.

Meri picked at her lavender fingernail polish. "I think they were hired to watch me, more than protect me," she confessed at last. "To make sure I didn't do something stupid that could embarrass my mom and ruin her chances."

Sudi stared at Meri, suddenly understanding how difficult Meri's life must be. Meri shrugged as if Sudi's pity made her uncomfortable. "You get used to it," Meri said, and then she asked, "So when did you realize that what Abdel told us was real?"

"I still don't believe it," Sudi said firmly and leaned over to roll up the cuffs. Then she slipped into the sweater. It smelled heavily of the last wearer's sharp perfume. She lifted her hair from underneath the turtleneck and let it hang loosely over her shoulders.

"I keep denying the truth, too," Meri confessed. "It's common. People convince themselves that unpleasant things aren't true so that they don't have to face their problems. Just watch the evening news. Politicians are always accusing each other of doing something wrong, when they should really be examining their own actions."

"There has to be a logical explanation," Sudi countered as she tied the shoelaces. "I just haven't found it yet." Sudi stood and tested the sneakers. They were a tad too large, and the insides felt grungy against her toes, but she was grateful to have something on her feet.

"I read a spell for transforming into a cat," Meri said at last. "Then I fell asleep, or at least I think I did, and when I woke up I was licking the back of my hand and rubbing it over my face."

Sudi looked up at the rectangle of blue sky between the office building and the school. *This can't be real,* she prayed. *Please don't let it be.*

"I think we should find Dalila," Meri said.

CHAPTER 8

By the time Sudi and Meri had located Dalila, through the Egyptian Cultural Center, the sun had set behind storm clouds. Dalila had agreed to meet them in an hour, but two had passed already. Sudi looked down the street. The traffic lights changed from red to green, the pedestrian signal counting down the seconds left to cross the street.

"She's still not answering." Meri closed her cell phone. "I hope she didn't change her mind."

"I wish she'd hurry," Sudi mumbled and brushed a yellow leaf from her wind-tangled hair.

This section of the District was crowded during the day, but it emptied after the offices closed. Even the eateries had turned out their lights. Still, Sudi didn't understand why she felt so uneasy. She had been there at night before, with Sara, when they had snuck out to go to an underground club called the Breeze.

"Scott likes you, you know?" Meri said abruptly, surprising Sudi.

"Scott?" Sudi stuttered. "I didn't know you knew him."

"We hang out," Meri said. "He was really bummed when you started going out with Brian, because he thought you liked him."

"I do like Scott," Sudi answered and started to explain, but stopped. "I see Dalila."

Dalila ran through tumbling leaves, her long coat flapping behind her. She held the rolled papyrus close to her chest as she joined them.

"I'm sorry I'm late," Dalila said. Her fingers plucked at the red scarf wrapped around her head, pulling it forward, as if she were afraid to reveal her royal birthmark. "I couldn't figure out how to work the machine to buy a ticket for the Metro, so I had to walk."

"Why didn't you just ask someone for help?" Meri said.

"Because, since my uncle told me that everything Abdel said was true, I've been too afraid to trust anyone," Dalila confessed.

"Who is your uncle?" Sudi asked.

"Anwar Serenptah," Dalila answered.

"Jeez, maybe he's the one we need to talk to," Meri said. "He's about the most famous Egyptologist in the world."

"Exactly," Dalila went on. "But he's misled me. He must have known that I didn't understand what it meant to be a Descendant. He swore that he thought my parents had told me. How could he believe that? I'm always looking through bridal magazines and planning my royal wedding. If I had any notion that I was going to be a warrior, I would have been learning how to fire a gun. He let me believe my fantasy. Why did he deceive me?"

Her face crumpled, the lines expressing terrible loss, and for a moment Sudi thought Dalila was going to cry, but she remained stubbornly strong.

"I understood that I was being groomed for something special," Dalila continued, "because I live such a sheltered life. But I thought I was destined to marry a prince. I imagined myself becoming like Queen Noor of Jordan, not a soldier fighting ancient gods. I can't do this."

Sudi put her arm around Dalila and hugged her. She was the only fifteen-year-old girl Sudi knew who really believed she'd marry a prince.

"My uncle taught me the ancient ways in magic and religion," Dalila said. "But I thought he was only sharing his love for Egypt with me, not training me."

"Has anything bizarre happened to you?" Sudi asked.

"No," Dalila answered, obviously lying. She tightened her grip on the papyrus. "Why do you ask?"

"Because," Sudi hesitated, then decided the best way to begin was to tell Dalila everything.

Recalling the night she had awakened and found herself on the front porch, Sudi began. She told Dalila about the invitation she had found in her locker and ended with her time spent trapped inside the museum.

When Sudi finished, she expected Dalila to give her a rush of possibilities to explain away what had happened, but she didn't.

"Maybe it was the Noble Lady," Dalila offered. "The demon Shepeset is like a fairy godmother. She was obviously protecting you. Demons can be good or bad; some offer protection, some don't."

"The Noble Lady," Meri repeated, eyeing Dalila quizzically. "You think the woman was a demon called Shepeset and not a creation of Sudi's overactive imagination?"

"Maybe hallucinations are just another reality that we don't see most of the time." Dalila shrugged.

"You believe everything I told you, don't you?" Sudi asked, mystified. This was not the reaction she had anticipated. Dalila's ability to believe her was making Sudi uncomfortable.

"Perhaps good forces sealed the elevator as a

way to protect you," Dalila explained. "What if the woman wanted to stop you from sleepwalking outside again, and trapping you in the museum was the only way she knew to keep you safe?"

"You accept this so easily," Meri put in.

"An unseen world surrounds us," Dalila said, "and it became visible to Sudi last night."

Warm rain splattered their faces, but they didn't run for shelter. They stayed in the downpour, staring at each other. Sudi pressed her lips together, feeling a sudden overwhelming sadness. Her future was going to be far different from the one she had planned. Already she could feel her friendship with Sara drifting into the past, and that loss made her chest ache.

At school, Sudi basically ignored the goodie girls, because she had nothing in common with them, and now she was stuck with two of them. Meri had probably never even tasted beer, and she looked too serious to fall into a goofy giggling spell the way Sudi and Sara did. Dalila was gorgeous, but seemed too bookish, and she had lived isolated from kids her own age, content with imagining the desert kingdom she would rule one day.

Sudi wondered if they ever even thought about boyfriends and dating or sex—things Sudi spent most of her time thinking about. She'd have to watch what she said in front of them. No more squealing over some good-looking guy's butt. She missed Sara already.

Then she realized that Dalila and Meri had become strangely quiet and were looking at her.

"I'm smart," Sudi blurted out defensively. She hated being stereotyped, even when she knew she was guilty of judging them.

"Why did you say that?" Meri asked, wiping the rain from her face.

"Of course you're smart," Dalila answered. "You're a Descendant."

They watched Sudi, and another awkward silence settled over the three girls.

"This is not the way to start off," Sudi said at last. "Let's just forget I said anything."

Dalila smiled pleasantly, but Meri frowned.

"Things like this don't happen," Sudi went on. "There has to be a reasonable explanation. We'll find it, and then we can separate and go back to our normal lives."

"Assume it's real," Meri said.

"I can't," Sudi answered in a low voice and licked at the rain on her lips.

"Just assume," Meri said, "if it's real, then we have to tell Abdel we're not going to take on this job as Descendants. He can't force us to fight against our will."

The idea had never occurred to Sudi. "You're right!" she shouted. Her chest expanded as the anxiety that had been holding her eased. "We'll just tell him we want out."

Dalila brightened. "I know where he lives. Let's go there right now and be done with this."

They linked arms and ran across the street. As they passed an alley, Meri stopped and looked around, cupping her hands around her forehead to shield her eyes from the rain.

"What's wrong?" Sudi asked, and felt the peculiar drop in her stomach that she got before tests.

"I don't know, I just . . ." Meri stared across the street at an empty black sedan. The raindrops on her face sparkled red, reflecting the light from the neon sign buzzing overhead. "Ever since my mother declared herself a candidate for president I've had photographers stalking me."

"Did you hear that?" Dalila asked and hooked her arm around Sudi's elbow.

"What?" Sudi listened to the pattering rain, and then, over the burble of water, came a sharp howl, followed by two longer cries.

"The cry of the jackal," Dalila whispered, pressing closer to Sudi. "We heard the jackals calling to each other when we camped on the west bank of the Nile. Jackals always howl before they begin their hunt."

"This is Washington, D.C.," Meri countered.

"The jackals cried the evening my parents were killed in the cave-in," Dalila went on. "My parents were excavating a tomb, and a tunnel collapsed on them."

"Maybe we should go back the other way," Meri suggested, nervously scanning the alleyway.

"It's just a dog," Sudi said, trying to reassure them. "It's probably lost and hungry." She started forward, intending to rescue the poor animal, but Meri latched on to her arm and pulled her back.

"The howls sound human," Meri said. "Maybe it's some guy—"

Another wail interrupted her. The mournful cry seemed closer, but with the noise from the rain, Sudi couldn't be sure.

"I've got a creepy feeling it's someone from the homeless shelter who's having a breakdown," Meri whispered.

"No," Dalila muttered and stepped back.

"What now?" Sudi asked, and brushed her hair from her eyes. She couldn't see what held Dalila's frightened gaze.

Meri pointed. "There!"

A shadow darted from behind a forklift stacked high with pallets and disappeared again, hidden by darkness and rain.

"That was Anubis, Neb-ta-djeser, lord of the sacred land," Dalila said. Her fingers fumbled with the papyrus as she tried to open it. "He has power over evildoers and the underworld enemies of the dead." She unrolled the scroll. "Help me find a spell."

"Don't be so panicked," Sudi said, not understanding her friends' fear. "It's just a dog, and

I bet it's more afraid of us than we are of it."

Sudi tried to see the animal, but the falling rain reflected the light cast from a security lamp, and the glistening drops acted as a shield, hiding the deeper shadows at the end of the alley.

This time Sudi ignored Dalila and Meri when they tried to stop her. She stepped forward until the brightness was behind her. Then she waited for her eyes to adjust to the dark, but before the moment came, a low growl filled the air and she realized her mistake. She was backlit by the security light, a silhouette easily spotted.

She hadn't thought this through; she had failed to consider that the dog might be rabid, or worse; maybe it was a military animal, one trained to kill, that had escaped its handlers. She imagined sharp teeth biting into her skin and instinctively pulled her sweater collar up around her neck.

Another howl pierced the night, and then, without warning, something splashed through water at a quickening pace, charging toward her.

Sudi darted forward. Her fingers brushed over the rough bricks in the building as she ran through the runoff water. The insides of her shoes became uncomfortably soggy.

She edged against the wall, her heart pounding painfully. Her shoulder slipped into a recess, and she quickly eased into the alcove behind her, then squatted against the door, trying to make herself small and less noticeable.

Through the pelting rain came another sound. She listened intently, trying to make sense of the tap-tapping. Perhaps a cane, or a baseball bat, was hitting the pavement with a repeated beat. A dog couldn't do that. Maybe Meri had been right after all, and the howls had come from a man.

Sudi's eyes had adjusted to the gloom, and she looked frantically around for another hiding place. Beyond the veil of water, a short ladder led to a loading deck. She ran to it and climbed up, her shoes slipping on the rungs. She caught movement in her peripheral vision, and dived behind crates that were stacked high. She prayed that whoever was pursuing her hadn't seen her hide, but she wasn't taking any chances. She crawled to the other side of the platform, then waited, shivering and terrified.

The tapping stopped, as if the person had paused, listening, waiting for her to make another sound.

She held her breath, her heartbeat thudding in her ears.

Moments passed with only the pulse of the rain and her heart, and then a scraping sound followed; someone was moving the crates aside, trying to locate her.

Any remaining illusion that a dog was hunting her vanished as she watched three crates topple. The person had to be high on PCP to have such strength. She rolled to the edge of the platform, dangled her feet over the side, and jumped, then crouched low.

Gushing waters swirled around her ankles before gurgling down a drain. She looked around and then ran across the alley to a truck. She slid under the front bumper, scraping her stomach on grit and dirt. She cowered behind the front wheel and hoped it hid her.

Within moments, the tapping started again, but the constant patter of the rain made it difficult for her to know how close her stalker was. She started to peer out.

The tip of a rod came down in front of her, barely missing her face. It hit the pavement with a loud bang.

She jerked back and waited, unable to breathe.

A bare foot splashed into a puddle, sending grimy water over her face. The person continued around to the side of the truck.

She pulled herself forward until she was under the bumper, then cautiously crawled out and, holding on to the front grille, peered around the truck.

A huge man stood in the rain. His legs were bare up to his knees. A soggy white skirt clung to his thighs, but nothing covered his back. He carried a large walking stick that looked like the snake she had found on her bed.

She brushed the rain from her face, certain her vision had deceived her, and looked again. Sudden intense terror shot through her. Her stomach tightened, and in spite of the water everywhere, her throat became too dry to swallow. She held her breath, transfixed, unmindful of the rain pelting her eyes.

The man was wearing a headdress—a full

head mask of a black dog with slender, alert ears and a long, pointed snout like that of the canine that had gazed back at her through the kitchen window. A thick mane of black hair covered his shoulders.

Slowly, the head turned, as if the man had become aware of her watching him.

Sudi sucked in air and let it out in a mumbled prayer.

A low, rumbling, growl issued forth from the man's throat. He stepped toward her before she could move. His walking stick swung around, the snake head aimed at her face.

She ducked, then scrambled on her hands and knees through the puddles back toward Dalila and Meri, too terrified to scream. She managed to stand, then ran, skidding once on the wet, oil-slick pavement.

The man seized her with unimaginable strength and lifted her, using only one hand. She sensed he was going to fling her to the ground. She tried to hold on to his back. Her palm slid up his shoulder, through the mass of black hair to the back of his head.

She felt no seam, no break, and where there should have been a dividing point between his body and the headdress, unless the man actually had a dog's head. She refused to accept what her mind was thinking, what she knew was fact.

The man yanked her forward. When she felt him start to throw her down, she grabbed the snout of his mask. Her hand slipped into his mouth. Her fingers traced over a warm, slippery tongue and teeth, but worse was the carrion stench of his panting breath and the sticky saliva that clung to her skin.

He hurled her to the ground, and she landed hard on her side.

"Don't let him point the walking stick at you!" Dalila shouted, charging toward her. The red scarf had slipped, revealing her royal birthmark.

Sudi let her head fall back on the pavement. "Right," she moaned, struggling to get away as the man reached for her again and started to pick her up.

"Stop!" Meri screamed and ran at him. Her feet splashed water into Sudi's face as she charged the creature.

Sudi jumped up in spite of the pain and

dizziness. She struggled forward and caught Meri, pulling her back.

"He's real," Sudi said jaggedly. "He's not a man wearing a costume."

Meri whipped around, her head bumping into Sudi's chin, and she stared up at Sudi, her eyes widening and terror-struck.

"He's the jackal-headed god Anubis," Dalila explained.

Anubis turned his attention away from Sudi and regarded Dalila, seeming to stare at the birthmark on her scalp. He snarled threateningly.

The three girls eased back, then stood, huddled together, in front of Anubis. Meri's teeth chattered. Dalila raised the papyrus in front of them. "We'll call forth the magical protection of the goddess Ipy," Dalila explained and pointed to a line of hieroglyphs. "The goddess Ipet."

"Ipy or Ipet?" Meri asked.

"It's the same goddess," Dalila answered. "Different names."

Rain splattered the papyrus, and the colors began to run together.

"Other gods fall down in terror before

Anubis," Dalila said. "But Ipy will stand against Anubis and protect us."

"How are you going to call a god?" Sudi asked, unable to control the trembling in her knees.

"Medu neter," Dalila said.

"What?" Meri asked.

"Divine words," Dalila said and pointed to the hieroglyphs again. "We'll use the words that our ancestors spoke." She cleared her throat and began, "Mistress of magical protection, Ipet-weret, the great Ipet, we call you forward."

Meri spoke the spell with her.

Anubis started toward them again. His yellow eyes focused on Sudi.

Sudi pinched the edge of the scroll and tried to work her tongue around the foreign words. Terror made her speak louder than both Meri and Dalila combined. "Thy hidden name we use," Sudi said. Her throat and mouth burned as she spoke the secret name of Ra, and then at the end of the incantation she added, "To call forth Ihy."

Dalila turned, her eyes stricken with horror. "You spoke the wrong name."

"I said Itchy or Ithy," Sudi said defensively. "Whatever you said, that's what I said."

"No, you didn't," Dalila argued. "You said Ihy, not Ipy or Ipet."

"Are we going to argue about that now?" Meri asked. "Find another spell, and hurry."

A rattling sound made Sudi look behind her. She saw nothing. Maybe it had only been her nerves, but the short, sharp jangle repeated, and something touched the back of her jeans. She looked down.

A naked boy stood behind her, shaking a sistrum. He waved the wooden handle, and the metal rods slid from side to side, making a tinkling noise. His head had been shaved except for one black lock, and he was sucking his free thumb.

"That's the god we summoned to protect us?" Sudi asked, dismayed.

"That's the one you called forth," Dalila answered. "Not us. That's the child-god Ihy. His musical instruments make people fall in love. He can't fight a death god."

The boy looked up at Sudi with a naughty sparkle in his eyes and rattled his sistrum, before he gazed behind her and saw Anubis. He screamed and ran off, his bare feet smacking against the rain-slick pavement.

Sudi turned as Anubis lifted the walking stick and pointed it at her. She sensed something dreadful building in the air. The rain stopped falling around the tip and slid to the sides as if the power circling it were too dense for even water to penetrate.

"What's he doing with his walking stick?" Sudi asked.

"It's not a walking stick," Dalila corrected. "It's a magic wand. Ancient Egyptians used wands to command malevolent spirits and demons."

"Is that what he thinks we are?" Meri asked, clutching Sudi's arm.

"Of course not," Dalila answered, her head bent over the soggy scroll, trying to find another spell. "He's going to use magic to destroy us."

CHAPTER 9

The earth rumbled, and the pavement cracked. Bricks snapped beneath Sudi's feet. She lost her balance, and as she started to fall, a deep, steep-sided hole opened in front of her. She remained suspended on the edge, and then the alley tilted and she plummeted into the abyss, her stomach turning from the rapid fall.

Meri and Dalila spun after her, their screams rising along with Sudi's piercing shriek. Clods of dirt and broken bricks tumbled over them, and then the ground overhead closed, sealing them in the dark chasm.

Soon moist, sticky-cold air gave way to intense heat, and just when Sudi thought she'd pass out, the free fall ended and her feet came down, settling on whitewashed limestone.

She blinked at the sudden brightness, and as her eyes adjusted, she saw shadows scampering about and hiding.

"Where are we?" she asked, her voice echoing around her as if she were in a vast, empty tunnel.

"Surely not under the earth," Meri said.

"We're standing at the entrance to—" Dalila started to answer, but before she could finish, another force washed over them, tightening its hold.

They shot forward.

In front of them, two monumental lions were joined back to back, guarding a gateway. The head of one giant statue faced east, the other, west.

"It's the first hour," Dalila screamed, and the red scarf that had been tied around her head whipped free.

"What?" Sudi yelled back.

"We passed the gate which swallows all," Dalila answered, clutching the papyrus close to her body with one hand and trying to grab on to the wall with the other. Her fingers thumped against the next gateway, but the pain didn't stop her from trying again.

"Where are we?" Sudi repeated her question.

"We passed the entrance to Duat," Dalila warned. "We're in the other world."

"Do you mean hell?" Meri shouted.

"We have to stop whatever is dragging us through the gates," Dalila said. "Once we pass the last pylon we'll enter eternity, and we won't be able to return."

Sudi flung her hands out and tried to hold on, hoping to catch a ledge, or protruding stone. Her fingernails scraped along the wall, and then the nail bed on her pinkie tore.

Unexpectedly, they stopped again, their feet landing softly on the stone floor.

"What now?" Sudi asked, and braced herself against the wall.

Dalila placed her hand against Sudi's mouth and looked around, her eyes alert.

Then Sudi heard the scuffing sound. Something large scraped furtively across the floor, coming toward them.

"What is it?" Meri said in a soft voice.

"Did we pass the seventh gate?" Dalila whispered anxiously. "I should have counted, but I didn't."

Sudi and Meri shrugged, and together they stepped away from the wall, Dalila between them, and stopped.

A huge snake slid toward them, leaving a frothy track of scum on either side of its massive body. It slithered forward, eyes filled with a killer's lust. Sudi couldn't see an end to its long, cylindrical body. It curled around column after column, seeming to fill the room.

"The fiend of darkness," Dalila whispered. "It's the soul-hunting demon, Apep. He'll take our souls."

An aura of evil pulsed from the serpent, and Sudi could feel its hatred for her. Even so, she couldn't pull her eyes away. Its gaze held her spellbound, tugging her forward, entrancing her and inviting her in to its widening mouth.

"Do something," Meri said. "Find a spell."

Dalila held up the dripping papyrus and unrolled the mushy scroll. The colors had run together, and the hieroglyphs now looked like blotches in a finger painting.

The giant serpent squirmed closer, its underbelly slipping over the steps with a wet, plopping sound.

Tears filled Sudi's eyes as all of her dreams fell away; she had never thought she would die so young.

"Don't cry," Meri said and pinched Sudi. "You have to help get us out of here. I'm not ready to die. I haven't even kissed a guy yet, and half my friends back home are seriously discussing birth control."

Sudi's head whipped around. "You haven't been kissed?" she asked, breaking out of her trance. "Never?"

"Would I lie to you, now?" Meri asked.

"A bird can escape," Dalila said and clasped Sudi's arm. "I'm sure that's what my uncle told me. A bird can fly out of Duat, because it can rise above Apep. Turn into the Bennu-bird, and you'll have the strength to carry us out."

"Fly out of here?" Sudi asked. "How? We're sealed underground."

"Just try," Meri pleaded.

Apep roared as if it understood what Sudi was about to do. It pulled its head back, ready to strike.

Sudi spoke the incantation three times and began flapping her arms, as feathers sprouted through her skin. Soon, huge, graceful wings stirred the air, but she didn't fly. She needed the help of the wind.

Dalila seemed to understand and began spinning. She raised one hand above her head, leaving the other down, and continued circling. "The breath of the gods, comforting and warm," Dalila spoke. "Bring your gift to lift Sudi's wings."

Suddenly, a breeze fluttered, following the direction of Dalila's dance. Meri joined her, clumsily at first, and then with grace, and they twirled together.

The wind lifted Sudi's wings. Dalila and Meri ran after her and grabbed on to her tail feathers, but Sudi didn't feel pain the way she had when her sister Nicole had stepped on her wing. She felt strong.

"*Neteri kua.* I am strong," she chirped.

Apep struck, but missed, then pulled back to strike again, and bellowed when Sudi soared away.

Sudi glided through the gateway, the tailwinds pushing her forward. She flew past the lion statues and then ascended with incredible speed, blindly flapping her wings.

Without warning, they burst through into the muggy night, landing back in Washington, D.C., on the steps of the FBI building.

Sudi moaned, a girl again, but racked with pain, unable to move. She lay on the concrete, smelling the rain and staring up at the night, watching the ragged low clouds skating across the sky beneath the larger and darker thunderheads.

"They probably caught all that on closed-circuit TV," Sudi said. "But I'd rather face an FBI agent than that snake."

"At least it wasn't a giant insect. I would have died," Meri exclaimed. "I hate bugs more than anything in the world."

Dalila sighed. "This is worse than I ever could have imagined," she said solemnly. "I probably won't even live long enough to become a bride."

"But we're okay right now," Meri said, sitting up.

"Because Dalila saved us with her dance," Sudi said. "How did you do that?"

"It's simple," Dalila explained. "All natural phenomena are manifestations of the divine, and if you concentrate hard enough, and the gods bless you for your devotion, the wind will come to you."

"Dalila, you're the perfect Descendant," Sudi said, slowly pulling herself up. "But I don't think I have a chance. It's not like the Book of Thoth makes us invincible and calling forth the protection of an ancient god is hard."

"I know," Dalila agreed sadly. "Egyptians worshipped hundreds of deities, and a slip of the tongue can summon the wrong one, as we found out when we called forth the child-god Ihy, instead of the protector goddess Ipy."

"You also called her Ipet-weret," Meri said. "Why did you use the other name?"

"That's just one more problem," Dalila explained "Even the names of the gods are confusing, because they have the Greek name, the Egyptian name, and the Roman name, and probably names I don't even know, because some were worshipped in Mesopotamia."

Dalila became silent, staring down at the scrapes and cuts on her right hand. The bruised knuckles were swelling.

"What is it?" Sudi asked with renewed apprehension.

"I was thinking about the jackal-headed god," she said. "Anubis was once the most important Egyptian funerary god. That is, until his cult was taken over by the priests devoted to Osiris; but some of the priests who served Anubis didn't want to lose their power, so they desecrated the temple and used Anubis and the Book of Gates in unholy ways to call forth demons and resurrect the dead."

"Did your uncle tell you that?" Meri asked.

"Many times," Dalila replied, "but until now I thought it was only part of mythology, not history."

Sudi edged closer to Dalila and put her hand on her shoulder, sensing that fear was making Dalila hold back something important. "What else did your uncle tell you?"

For a long time Dalila stared at the leaves skittering across the street, and then she spoke. "The

Cult of Anubis wants to return the universe to the chaos from which it came, and now they worship the ancient god Seth." She looked from Sudi to Meri and back to Sudi again. "I don't see how we can survive."

"We'll spend the night together at my house," Sudi said firmly. "Then, tomorrow, we'll find Abdel and tell him we want out."

CHAPTER 10

"You've got to see this," Dalila yelled the next morning as Sudi entered the bedroom, carefully balancing three cups of hot cocoa on a tray.

Meri and Dalila were already dressed in clothes they had borrowed from Sudi's closet. They stood at her window, watching Pie. The old yellow tomcat stretched in the sunlight, his back paws on the windowsill, forepaws wrapped around the lock.

"Pie thinks you've been careless," Meri said. "You need to lock your window at night, because evil things have been hanging out in your backyard."

Sudi set the tray down and grabbed Pie, rolling him into a ball and rubbing her nose against his. "Are you part of the feline underground?" she joked.

Pie looked at her with a slight nod of his head, and for the briefest moment Sudi felt that her pet had understood her. She set him down on the floor, and just when she decided that she had only imagined him nodding, Patty Pie meowed.

Meri took her cup of cocoa and poked at the marshmallow with her finger, watching Pie. "He says the cherry-vanilla ice cream you've been feeding him is too sweet and he wants you to buy chocolate next time."

Sudi paused. "You really are communicating with Pie," she said in wonder.

Meri nodded.

Dalila glanced at her watch. "We'd better get going."

The girls finished their cocoa, and then they

headed downstairs, stealing past the kitchen. Sudi glanced into the room. Nicole was crushing potato chips between two slices of white bread covered with globs of mayonnaise. Their mother stood next to Nicole, staring out the kitchen window and drinking her morning coffee.

Sudi hurried outside and didn't turn back when her mother called after her. She was determined to end whatever it was that Abdel had started.

Six blocks later, Dalila, Meri, and Sudi stood on a cobblestone street in Georgetown, staring up through red maple leaves at a yellow row house.

"This is where my uncle brought me," Dalila said. "He told me Abdel belonged to a secret society called the Hour priests. I had never seen my uncle so excited to meet anyone before, and he's met a lot of famous people."

Sudi walked up the iron steps, the metal clanging beneath her boots, and knocked on the door.

Abdel opened it.

"You're here," he whispered, seeming surprised. "I've been trying to find all three of you."

"We want out," Sudi said, barging inside. She

turned to face him. "You need to find someone more mature, someone with military training. Maybe the whole U.S. Marine Corps!"

"No way are we doing this," Meri added, joining Sudi.

Dalila shut the door behind her. "How can I fight demons?" she demanded. "I don't even know how to ride the Metro."

"There's nothing I can do to change your fate," Abdel answered calmly.

"It's never too late," Meri said. "Besides, you had the responsibility to explain everything to us and you failed."

"You failed big-time," Sudi added.

"I'm probably not the best priest to advise you in this battle," Abdel confessed, "but I am the only one you have."

"Battle?" Dalila looked suddenly pale. "I learned the proper way to bow to kings," she went on in a thin voice. "I know how to receive diplomats, but I never learned how to fight."

"Please," Sudi said. Her throat burned as anger rose to cover her feelings of helplessness. Her sisters were probably the ones he wanted anyway, but she definitely wasn't going to mention that and put the twins in danger. They were too careless as it was.

"You don't understand how this could hurt my mom," Meri added. "She wants to run for president."

"It's too late," Abdel answered. "You left me before I was able to explain the spells on your papyri—"

"That's not our fault," Meri interrupted, angrily. "You were scaring us."

"The ceremony was needed to awaken your divine spirits," Abdel countered.

Sudi looked at the overstuffed armchairs in the living room. "You should have brought us here and told us everything."

"You never would have come," Abdel answered. "But I knew you wouldn't refuse an invitation to the Sky Terrace restaurant, and none of you did. My only mistake was in assuming that the three of you would listen to me until I had finished telling you everything you needed to know."

"Any rational person would have left long before we did," Meri charged.

"Even so, I can't do anything to change what

has happened," Abdel said and leaned back against a table near the door. "I can see the difference in your eyes, and I know that each of you has already accepted her fate."

"We did not agree to this," Dalila said.

"But you did," Abdel answered. "You've used the spell to awaken your power of transmutation."

"Our what?" Sudi asked.

"Like Horus, who could transform into a falcon and fly over his kingdom, each Descendant has the ability to change into an animal. That power came alive when you recited the proper spell from your papyrus. Once the spell is spoken, the ability remains for life, and by speaking the incantation you accepted your destiny. Usually it's done in a ceremony—"

"It's not like I knew what I was doing," Meri said. "I ate a mouse! Do you really think I wanted to do that?"

"And my cat almost ate me," Sudi added. "I hate being a bird. It's scary to fly so high."

Dalila hesitated, then pressed her hands against her cheeks. "I turn into Ammut, the monster with the head of a crocodile and the forepaws of a lion. I have the hindquarters of a hippopotamus. How am I ever going to find a husband looking like that?"

"Dalila," Abdel said gently. "You're supposed to turn into a fire-breathing cobra like the goddess Wadjet. You must yield to your power and not be afraid. You're limiting yourself and not becoming what you were meant to be because of your disbelief and fear."

"I can't do this." Dalila leaned against Sudi. "Don't you see? You're sending us to our deaths."

No one spoke for a long moment. Sudi felt defeated. Dalila's soft crying was the only sound in the gloomy room.

Finally, Abdel spoke. "As long as all three of you are here, we should begin your training."

"We refuse," Sudi answered with a bravery she did not feel. "You'll have to find others."

Abdel started up the steep stairs anyway, the old wood creaking under his weight. When he reached the first landing, he turned back and looked down at them.

"The longer you wait to learn what you need to know, the longer you will live in terrible danger.

The cult doesn't care that you don't want to fulfill your destiny. The leaders will send demons to kill you, and if you're not concerned for your own safety, then at least consider the welfare of your families."

"Our families," all three girls said as one.

Sudi couldn't let anything happen to her sisters or her parents. She clutched the newel post. "I don't know if I can," she said, her stomach churning.

"It's hard," Abdel whispered. "No one would freely choose the life you have been given."

Sudi started up the stairs. Meri and Dalila followed after her with slow, reluctant steps.

"You tricked us," Sudi said when she reached Abdel. "You gave us the scrolls with the right incantations knowing we would speak them."

"That deception has been done before." Abdel nodded, but he didn't seem to take any joy in his trickery. "I knew that once I had awakened the soul of Egypt within you, destiny would find a way to make you read the incantation and bind your fate to that of a Descendant."

On the third floor, Abdel took a large key from his pocket and undid the lock on a door with three clicking turns. He pushed the door open and stepped into a dark, stuffy room.

A flame flared, and Sudi watched as Abdel continued to light the white wicks floating inside oil-filled clay bowls. When he finished, twenty or more flames flickered, and a soft haze hung in the stale air.

"Please, take a seat," he said when he noticed that they were still standing in the doorway.

The girls circled a low, round table in the center of the room and sat down on roughly made stools.

Abdel set a copper chest on the table, opened it, and took out three cylindrical leather cases. "This is only the first of many from the Book of Thoth that you will be required to study." He reached inside the first worn pouch and carefully pulled out a scroll.

"The secrets of the gods, written by Djehuti," Dalila whispered, and reverentially touched the tattered papyrus. "The Book of Thoth is mentioned in many papyri, but no copy has ever been found by archaeologists. Scholars thought all copies were lost in the fire that destroyed the library in Alexandria."

"The Hour priests have kept the scrolls hidden to protect the knowledge written on them," Abdel explained, "because whoever possesses the Book of Thoth has the power to command the gods of ancient Egypt, and even understand the language of animals and fly through the night unseen. Of course, there are risks."

"Great," Meri said and folded her arms.

Abdel sat down, seeming pleased with himself. "Now I will take you back with a story to the beginning of time," he announced, "so you will know your enemy. Many myths are told to explain creation, but all stories originate with the primeval waters and the mound which rose from them. The story I tell you is the true one."

He paused as if he were beginning the recitation of a text he had memorized as a boy. "From the primordial waters of chaos came the mound of creation, and on it sat Amun-Re. The great god brought forth life, and, soon after, the opposing gods of order and chaos, Osiris and Seth, were born."

Sudi had an odd feeling that she wasn't in the row house anymore, but when she glanced around, she saw the same tall bookcases, the flickering flames, and the thin smoke rising to the ceiling.

"Osiris married the goddess Isis," Abdel continued, "and together they ruled Egypt and brought order to the land. Isis was a devoted and faithful wife. Everyone loved her. But the evil god Seth grew jealous of his brother's good fortune. He killed Osiris and seized the throne."

Abdel shuddered as if he had witnessed the crime. "Grief-stricken, Isis stole the Book of Thoth from the gods and used its magic to resurrect Osiris long enough to conceive an heir, a son named Horus.

"When Horus came of age, he challenged his uncle Seth, and, after much struggle, the gods declared that Horus was the true pharaoh. Isis had her revenge, but she feared Seth would retaliate by freeing the demons that lived in the chaos at the edge of the universe."

Abdel looked at each of the girls to make sure he had their full attention before he continued. "For that reason, Isis gave the Book of Thoth to the Hour priests and directed them to watch the night skies. When the stars warned of evil forces threatening the kingdom, the priests were instructed to give the Book of Thoth to the pharaoh so he could use its magic to protect the world."

"That is why I am here," Abdel said. "The stars are warning of terrible days ahead unless the Cult of Anubis is stopped."

He glanced up, and the firelight made his eyes glint. "No one can change your fate, not even the gods. You must stand against evil and protect the world. You are the Descendants of the great kings of Egypt."

Sudi cursed under her breath and slouched against the table. Her throat tightened as daydreams of falling in love and losing her virginity were replaced by hideous kung fu images of running from monsters and losing her life.

CHAPTER 11

Blue smoke spiraled around the closed room, coming from incense burning within reddish gold plates. The scent settled over Sudi, too sweet and strong. She had worn a halter top, and the sticky vapor felt as if it were seeping into the bare skin of her arms and back. She wondered if kids at school could smell the cloying fragrance on her. For three weeks she had come to Abdel's house to read the Book of Thoth and memorize spells, but her thoughts kept jumping ahead to Michelle's party.

More than anything, Sudi wanted to go, but Abdel had told her it was too dangerous for her to be out at night until she learned more magic. She hadn't bothered to tell him that so far she hadn't memorized any spells. She glanced down at the invitation poking out of her backpack. Abdel wasn't her parent, so he couldn't actually keep her from going.

Everyone said Michelle's extravaganza was going to be the social event of the year. No one cared that it was on a school night, because Michelle's parents had hired Grammy-winner Sienna to sing, and Sunday night was the only time available in her frenzied schedule.

Sudi leaned back and opened the shutter, feeling the familiar longing to be outside. Meri's driver waited in the black Lincoln Continental parked at the curb. Red leaves from a maple tree fell on the car hood.

"Abdel is stifling our fun," Sudi blurted out.

"He's only being cautious," Dalila said, without looking up.

"If he really cares about us," Sudi argued, "then why does he always disappear when we come over here? I thought a mentor was supposed to guide us, not leave us in a stinking room with boring translations to do."

"I love doing this," Dalila said, and looked up this time. She smiled, as if studying were bliss.

"Some of us aren't scholars," Sudi explained.

"I hear footsteps upstairs," Meri put in. "I think Abdel stays nearby in case we do need him."

"Let's go somewhere," Sudi said. "We need a break."

"You don't understand the seriousness—" Dalila began.

"I think I know," Sudi snapped. "I'm the one who got jackal saliva all over her face."

Sudi regretted her outburst, but Dalila stood and began rolling up her papyrus. "You're right," Dalila said. "We need a break. Then we'll come back and study."

"Let's go to Dean & DeLuca," Sudi said, grabbing her backpack. "It's not far from here."

Meri started for the door. "My driver will take us."

A few minutes later, Sudi ordered a cappuccino at the outside counter of Dean & DeLuca. She breathed in the rich scent of coffee, then sipped the frothy milk from the top as she sauntered toward a table in the sunlight.

The sunshine warmed her bare arms and back, and she was glad she had worn the loose halter top. She dropped her backpack beside the metal chair, but just as she started to sit down, she saw Michelle push through the doors.

Michelle walked with an exaggerated swing of her hips, her feet coming down like a runway model's as she carried sandwiches to a table in the shade. Then Sudi saw the reason. Scott, Brian, and Carter lolled on the chairs. They wore shorts and long-sleeved rugby shirts with horizontal stripes in alternating blue and red. Brian's knee was bleeding, and he stretched his leg out into the aisle so that everyone passing could see the gash. Scott sat in a corner, his arm slung over the back of the chair. Sunglasses hid Carter's eyes, and even though he didn't wave, Sudi sensed that he was watching her.

"What's up?" Meri asked, setting her latte down and biting into a cookie.

"Carter told me that he played rugby with Scott, but I didn't know Brian played on the same team," Sudi said. "Do you think they talk?"

"About you?" Meri said with a teasing grin. "Sure, and right now Michelle is probably leading the conversation. She's so jealous."

Sudi glanced back. Michelle was standing behind Scott, rubbing his shoulders.

"Let's leave," Sudi said, grabbing the strap of her backpack.

Dalila surprised her by blocking her retreat. "You can't leave now."

"Why not?" Sudi asked.

"Because there are no coincidences," Dalila said, setting an espresso on the table. "Fate brought you here. Now be brave enough to see what destiny is going to offer you."

"My last big encounter with destiny was a jackal-headed god named Anubis," Sudi argued. "I don't think I want to know what providence is handing me today."

"Sit down," Meri said. "They probably won't even notice we're here."

Sudi slumped in her chair. Something tickled

her neck. She brushed back her hair, but instead of going away the feeling crawled across her collarbone. She scratched at her skin.

Meri sat straight up, jarring the table. Her eyes widened. "A bug," she said, pointing to Sudi's chest. "A really big bug. It's as long as my finger."

"It's a cicada," Dalila said, unconcerned. "Just flick it away."

"Get it off me!" Sudi cried.

"I hate bugs more than anything," Meri said. "I'm not going to touch it. What if it bites me?"

"Do cicadas bite?" Sudi asked and jumped up. Her chair scraped the ground with an ear-piercing shriek of metal legs on stone. If Brian, Carter, and Scott hadn't been aware of her presence before, they were definitely watching her now.

She slapped at her neck.

The frightened cicada flitted back and forth, then scrambled under her halter. Tiny, prickly insect feet scurried across her chest. The bug quivered and made a high-pitched, droning sound.

"Get it out. Get it out." Sudi grabbed the hem

of her halter and waved it up and down, trying to shoo the bug away.

Dalila jumped up, looking horrified.

"It's not a cicada after all, is it?" Sudi shouted, as new terror found her. From the shocked expression on Dalila's face, Sudi knew the insect was something poisonous.

"Stop!" Dalila yelled.

"What is it?" Sudi screamed and shook the halter vigorously, flapping it up and down. "Am I going to die?"

"Calm down," Dalila ordered and tried to grab Sudi's hands.

People gathered and looked alarmed. But no one stepped forward to save Sudi from the lethal insect.

"Help me," Sudi pleaded.

Then Scott pushed through the crowd. His hand darted forward, and his fingers brushed over Sudi's breast. He scooped the bug into his hand, then held it in his palm as if it were a pet.

"It's only a cicada," he said. "You don't need to be afraid."

"Put your top down," Dalila said, prying

Sudi's fingers from the hem of the halter.

Sudi gasped and let go. Finally, she understood.

"It's all right," Dalila whispered and went back to her seat.

Sudi smoothed her bodice, making sure the halter top covered her breasts. A blush burned her cheeks.

"A cicada can't hurt you," Scott continued. He tossed the broad-headed insect into the air. "It was probably afraid of you."

Sudi couldn't speak. She stared down at the ground, humiliated.

Scott leaned closer. "It's okay," he whispered into her ear. "I was getting a bug off of you, so it doesn't count."

She ventured a glance up, but Scott was already heading back to his seat. Carter stood in front of her.

"Great show," Carter said, lifting his sunglasses. "I'll definitely be there for your next performance."

He followed Scott back to their table.

People who had gathered to watch her hysterics smiled and dispersed.

Only Brian and Michelle remained.

"Nice try, Sudi," Brian said with a lopsided grin. "But even that show won't get me back."

"As if," Sudi answered, more flustered than before.

Meri pushed in front of Sudi. "Please. Why would she want you back?"

"Why wouldn't she?" Brian said with the conceit that Sudi had come to hate. He smirked and walked away.

"I can't believe you," Michelle said, fuming. "You were flashing Scott on purpose."

"I was attacked by a bug," Sudi said.

"Don't think for a minute that I believe you're afraid of a cicada. We used to catch them in my backyard, remember?"

Sudi started to defend herself, but stopped. "Whatever, Michelle."

"You're so déclassé," Michelle said. "Pathetic, really. I feel like taking back your invitation to my party."

Dalila stood up and slowly walked around the table. Her regal bearing made Michelle pause.

"Go back to pretending you're perfect," Dalila said with calm authority, "and let us drink our coffee without your rude comments."

Michelle stared at Dalila, but she didn't reply. She seemed suddenly unsure of herself and glanced at Sudi, then took two careful steps backward before hurrying back to her table.

"Can you believe she and I were once best friends?" Sudi asked.

"You're better off without her," Meri said. "She's such a poser."

"What do you suppose she's doing with them?" Sudi asked.

"Talking trash about you," Meri said and playfully nudged Sudi.

"At least now I don't have to figure out what to wear to the party tonight," Sudi said. "Because I'm definitely not going."

"We'll go with you," Dalila said, still gazing after Michelle.

"I can't face Scott," Sudi said.

"You're going," Meri said. "Because if you don't show up, then Michelle will think she's won."

"But you have to learn at least one incantation to stop an evil creature from attacking you," Dalila said.

"Just in case," Meri agreed.

"Nothing's going to happen at the party," Sudi said. She didn't want to go back to that dark little room with its smelly incense and lantern light.

"You need to know a spell," Meri persisted.

"Fine. I'll learn one," Sudi promised, even though she didn't sense any danger. Who was going to send a demon after her at a party where 300 people could witness the attack? The cult leaders wouldn't be that stupid. Besides she had watched enough scary movies to know the monsters would descend upon them, as before, when they were alone and vulnerable.

CHAPTER 12

One by one the wicks burned out. The dying flames sputtered and hissed, consuming the oil-soaked strips of cloth. Bitter smoke curled into the bluish incense vapors and rolled lazily about, fogging the air.

Sudi carried another copper trunk to the table. She opened it and pulled out a leather case, then blew away the sand and removed the papyrus. Dalila and Meri had left an hour ago, and Sudi still hadn't found the right spell. She needed to leave soon and get ready for the party.

Footsteps overhead startled her. She glanced at the ceiling. *Clunk. Thump.* The dull sounds repeated. What did Abdel do in the attic all day?

She refocused her attention on the papyrus and found an incantation for turning a demon into a small dog: *Goddess of magic, I entreat you, send a burning ring of fire around the one who beholds me. Set fire to his heart and change him into my dog.*

Sudi imagined the demon transforming into a Chihuahua. In her mind's eye, she saw the devil pup nipping at her heels and following her home. Carrie and Nicole would no doubt beg their mother to let them keep the dog, and the evil mutt would probably love the twins as much as it hated Sudi. She pictured it gnawing on her toes while she slept.

She shuddered and began searching for a spell that didn't turn the demon into a household pet.

A new heading caught her attention: *The Tricks of Love Divination.* Her heart raced. Did she dare?

A love spell appeared easy to cast. No ceremony was involved. She had only to recite the words. She pictured Scott falling for her and imagined his lips on hers, his hands . . . Why not? As long as she had to learn magic, she might as well practice on something fun.

The last flame burned out, leaving her in darkness. She opened a shutter, then grabbed a Sharpie from her backpack and, in the dim light cast by the streetlight, copied the love spell onto the inside of her right forearm.

"Goddess of magic, I entreat you." A pleasant feeling came over her as she began the incantation. "Send a burning ring of love fire around the one who beholds me. Set fire to his heart, that he might love me."

She needed another spell to stop evil, but for tonight the Chihuahua hex would have to do. Nothing was going to happen anyway. She quickly copied that incantation onto her left arm. She had to be careful not to confuse the two spells. They were almost the same, and she didn't want Scott to become her lapdog.

She grabbed her backpack and hurried down the stairs and out the front door. As she started home, she decided to wear her new push-up bra and the low-cut green top with the long sleeves that would hide the words written on her arms.

Two hours later, Sudi waited on the front lawn of Michelle's house, near the valets who had been hired to park the cars. Pink, orange, and gold lanterns swung from the oak trees, casting a fairy-tale glow over the yard. Music pulsed through Sudi. She couldn't wait to dance. It might have been Michelle's party, but Sudi felt as if she owned this night.

She stepped off the curb, loving the click of her heels on the pavement, and looked for headlights, anxious for Dalila and Meri to join her so she could go inside.

Finally, a black sedan pulled up. A valet opened the back door, and Meri jumped out, tugging at the hem of her black T-shirt. Silver sequins across the front spelled out PROBLEM CHILD. The low-slung jeans showed off her flat stomach.

Dalila scooted to the edge of the seat, then lifted her legs, pointed her toes, and alighted from the limo as if she had practiced being a queen a thousand times. Kohl darkened the rims of her eyelids, and a red sheath clung to her body. She touched Sudi's arm. Her cold fingers trembled. "I only know how to belly dance. I don't think I'll fit in here."

"We'll show you," Sudi said. "Let's go inside."
Sudi ran up the steps. She could feel the guys on
the veranda watching her. She squeezed in among
the dancers on the porch, and swept her hands up
her body in a flirty way, then arched her back and
ran her fingers through her thick blond hair. She
squealed and turned to bump hips with Meri and
Dalila—but instead she slid against air.

She glanced back at the lawn.

Dalila looked ready to run. Meri stood protec-
tively beside her.

Sudi hurried back down the steps and joined
them.

"You can't be that shy," Sudi said.

"If a boy touches me, I'll faint," Dalila said.
"Everyone dances so close."

"Here's a clue to get over your shyness," Sudi
said, hooking arms with Dalila and Meri and
pulling them forward. "It feels really, really good."

Sudi led them up the steps through the foyer
and into the living room. The music played loudly,
and a thrill rushed through her.

The furniture had been removed from the
rooms, and the walls and ceiling were covered with

sheer, gauzy fabric that swelled and rolled, changing shape continually and reflecting pink and orange lights. Sudi doubted that Michelle even knew all of the kids at the party—but she loved the way so many of them knew her, calling Sudi's name and asking her to join them.

She led Dalila and Meri past the dancers. When they rounded the corner, a fanfare of changing lights made her blink.

"Just how much money did Michelle's parents spend on this party?" Sudi asked, but then she saw Tyler and Jeff sitting at the bar, drinking sodas and eating peanuts. She didn't wait for an answer. "Those two are perfect," she said, and escorted Meri and Dalila forward.

Tyler and Jeff were juniors at Lincoln High, one year ahead of Sudi. She could see in their expressions that they recognized Meri. Then their gazes shifted to Dalila. Tyler slid from his stool and couldn't stop grinning. Jeff set his soft drink down and choked on a peanut. His brown hair fell in his eyes; he flipped it back with a nod of his head.

"Hey," Sudi said. "I want you to meet two of my best friends, Dalila and Meri."

"Hi," Tyler said, but his smile quickly faded into a look of concern.

Jeff stared at Meri, his puzzled expression growing into one of alarm.

Dalila turned first and let out a small scream. Then Sudi looked at Meri and gasped. Long feline whiskers had sprouted from Meri's cheeks.

Sudi stretched her arms to hide Meri from Tyler and Jeff. Then she and Dalila pulled Meri toward the bathroom.

"We'll catch you later," Sudi shouted over her shoulder.

"What are you doing?" Meri asked, a head shorter than she had been and shrinking. "I like Jeff."

"You've got cat ears poking out of your hair," Dalila said.

Meri shrieked and ducked low, pressing through the crush of dancers. A long tail wiggled from out of the top of her jeans.

When the bathroom door opened, Sudi, Dalila, and Meri dodged inside before the girls who had been waiting in line could stop them.

Sudi locked the door.

Meri jumped onto the counter near the sink and stared at her reflection. She patted her cheeks with the back of her hand to avoid scratching herself with her extended feline claws.

"I didn't say the incantation," Meri said when she was able to speak again. "So why is this happening?"

"Maybe nerves caused it," Sudi said, unable to pull her gaze away from Meri's unearthly beauty; the cat ears, whiskers, and changed eyes made Meri look like an enchantress from a fairy tale. "I'm sure we'll get control over the power in time."

Dalila began stoking Meri's hair, calming her. "Magic takes getting used to," Dalila soothed. "One day this will come naturally to you. It's like learning how to play a musical instrument. Mistakes are made at first." Slowly, Meri began changing back; the vertical pupils became black circles in the center of her eyes, whiskers disappeared leaving smooth skin, and the tail vanished.

Finally she slid off the counter, returned to her full girl size. "What if a photographer takes my picture and I end up some weird cat-freak girl on the cover of *Star*?"

"We'll deal with that if it happens," Sudi answered.

"I'm all right now," Meri said and took a deep breath before opening the door. "I'll concentrate on staying calm."

The three girls stepped toward the edge of the dancing crowd. The music pulsed around them and Sudi began to move, her eyes wandering, looking for Scott.

Jeff waved from across the room. He bumped around a line of dancers who were pressed together, moving back and forth in unison, and shoved his way toward Meri.

"Go dance with Jeff," Sudi said.

"Are you sure?" Meri said, waving back at Jeff.

"Go on," Sudi said, and mischievously pushed Meri toward Jeff. "Have fun."

When Sudi turned back, a flash of red among the dancers caught her attention. "I thought you said you couldn't dance," Sudi said and joined Dalila, bumping hips with her. "You're incredible. I want you to teach me."

Dalila swayed her body sensually, her shyness

gone. "I've been belly dancing since I was a little girl. It's in my blood."

All the guys began watching Sudi and Dalila dancing together, and then Carter stepped between them. He rested his hand on Sudi's shoulder, but he never stopped looking at Dalila.

"Introduce me to your friend, Sudi," he said.

"No, Carter," Sudi said harshly.

"What's wrong?" Dalila asked, and stared up at Carter like someone falling in love for the first time.

"Let's get some air," Sudi said but when she started to lead Dalila from the room, Carter put his arm around her friend, pulling her back to him.

"I'm not going to hurt her," he said to Sudi.

"Dalila doesn't know . . . she's lived a really protected life," Sudi argued.

"I'll watch over her," he insisted, gazing into Dalila's eyes. "I won't let anyone hurt her."

Dalila looked up at Carter with the same dreamy expression Sudi had seen on the faces of too many other girls. Sudi didn't understand their infatuations, and she couldn't comprehend how quickly Dalila had lost her shyness.

"I give you my word," Carter said. "Trust me, Sudi."

Carter tenderly kissed the top of Dalila's head before turning her around to face him. Maybe Carter was falling for Dalila. After all, she had been reared to enchant kings. Sudi watched as Carter guided Dalila outside and across the lawn to a stage that had been set up over the swimming pool.

Sudi followed them outside. The yard stretched on and on, sloping gently into a wooded area. She stepped onto the grass, and the aroma of chocolate drifted into the cool autumn night.

A buffet had been set up near the gazebo. The velvety candy dripped down three silver tiers into a huge bowl that was surrounded by fruit and marsh-mallows.

Sudi pushed into the group of kids gathered around the table and picked out a strawberry. Her mouth watered as she dunked it in the chocolate. But when she tried to ease away, a girl accidentally nudged her and Sudi stumbled into someone, dripping chocolate onto his shirt.

"Sorry," she said and looked up.

Brian glared down at her. "Real mature, Sudi. I know you did that on purpose."

Dominique tugged on Brian's sleeve. "She was only getting chocolate," Dominique said. "It was an accident."

"No, it wasn't," Brian argued. "She's desperate to get back with me."

Sudi rolled her eyes. "If I wanted you back," Sudi said, holding up the strawberry, "I think I could come up with a better scheme than this." She flicked more chocolate on him.

"Yeah," he blustered. "Like what you did earlier today."

Sudi hurried away as Brian started telling everyone the way she had flashed him at Dean & Deluca. Her perfect evening was spinning out of control. She sat down alone on a bench near the woods and stared at the rising moon, her back to the party. She licked at the chocolate on her fingers and wondered what she'd ever seen in Brian.

Someone tapped her shoulder. Before she could turn, Scott straddled the bench and sat beside her. His clothes smelled fresh and new, his aftershave musky.

"I was hoping you would still come tonight," he said.

She glanced down, suddenly self-conscious.

He touched her chin, lifting her head until she was forced to gaze into his eyes. "I barely looked," he teased. "Promise. So don't go shy on me."

Then he stood and took her hand, pulling her up to him. "Dance with me?" She could feel his desire; or was it her own? She started moving with him, enjoying the warmth of his body. His hand slipped down her back, and she caught her breath.

"I'm glad you broke up with Brian," he said, his minty breath mingling with hers.

"Me, too," she answered, and wondered if her eyes had the same dreamy expression that she had seen in Dalila's eyes.

"I'm the one you should have dated," he said, taking her hands and placing them around his neck. Then, his fingers caressed her waist and rested on her hips.

Maybe she wouldn't need to cast a spell on him after all.

She sensed someone watching her and glanced

back at the party, expecting to see Michelle glaring at her.

Instead, Michelle stood on the porch. Five guys crowded around her, all dressed in matching red shirts. Michelle's parents had hired professional dancers to make sure the party didn't lag. Sudi wondered if they had also hired escorts to hover around Michelle and give her a false sense of popularity.

The music changed. Michelle's entourage began clapping, and then all five broke into a hip-hop routine. Michelle danced with them, strutting and flaunting herself, moving toward the stage.

Sudi watched, stunned. "What is Michelle doing?"

"Michelle is Miss Diva," Scott said, his hand on Sudi's shoulder. "She's going to perform."

Sudi looked up at him, astonished. "I thought Sienna was singing."

"She is, but so is Michelle," Scott explained. "It's her special surprise for all her guests."

"I was hoping her special surprise was a goody bag," Sudi answered and stared back at Michelle, feeling sorry for her. "This is going to be a major embarrassment. Didn't anyone bother to tell Michelle that she can't sing?"

"I did," Scott said. "I was over here earlier listening to her rehearse. She's really bad. Carter and I tried to talk her out of it."

Sudi imagined that Brian had encouraged her so he could have a good laugh at Michelle's expense.

Kids began moving toward the stage, clapping and whistling, excited to see Sienna perform.

Two dancers lifted Michelle onto their shoulders. She must have thought all of the commotion was for her, because she smiled and waved, throwing kisses the way celebrities acknowledged cheering fans.

"I warned her," Scott said as he placed his arm around Sudi. "Come on."

Sudi had expected Scott to pull her toward the stage. Instead he steered her onto a path cut between the trees.

"What about Sienna? Don't you at least want to hear her sing?" Sudi asked.

"I can hear her anytime," Scott answered. "I have her CD. And I definitely don't want to listen to Michelle ruining my favorite songs."

"Is Michelle planning to sing *with* Sienna?" Sudi asked, surprised again. "Did Sienna agree to that?"

"I don't know," Scott said. "I have a feeling it's going to be a big surprise for her as well."

Sudi followed him down the path, crushing leaves under her shoes.

"Where are we going?" she asked.

"I want to show you something," he answered.

The thought of walking alone with him through the moonlit woods caused a pleasant chill to rush through her.

The party noise became muffled. Kids screamed and applauded, but the sound seemed far away. Minutes later, Sienna's sultry voice drifted into the night. Scott slowed his pace.

"What did you want to show me?" Sudi said breathlessly.

"This." He slipped both arms around her, and then bent down until she could feel his breath on her face. His lips lingered over hers, and when she didn't pull away, he kissed her.

Her stomach fluttered, and longing filled her body. Why had she wasted time with Brian? She wrapped her arms around Scott's waist and invited him closer, her hips slinking against him.

A twig snapped. She opened her eyes. A shadow slid from behind one tree to the next.

"It's probably only a rabbit," Scott said and nuzzled her neck.

But she had definitely seen something bigger than a rabbit move between the spindly trees. It was probably only a guy and a girl kissing in the shadows, the way they were.

Scott kissed her again, and this time she felt his tongue. She closed her eyes and relaxed in his arms.

A scuffling of leaves made her alert again. She pulled back. In the darkness beneath the trees, she spotted a lone figure, watching them.

"If you want to go slower, that's okay," Scott said, taking her hand. He started toward the path.

Sudi took a deep breath, trying to decide. The shadow was gone now. Maybe it had been nothing. But if the cult had sent a creature to harm her, she couldn't let it follow her back to the party, and she couldn't let Scott stay with her and put him in danger, either. She had to face whatever it was alone.

"Go back to the party without me," she said. "I'll catch up with you later."

"What?" He gave her a confused smile, as if he didn't understand her joke and was waiting for a punch line.

"I won't be long," she said and hurried away from him, ducking under low-hanging branches.

Mud sucked at her spiky heels, and she sank deeper with each step. Then, from behind her, came the sound of other footsteps squishing in the muck. She turned. Her heart raced, pumping adrenaline through her veins. The thin branches waved in front of her, snapping and breaking. She held her breath, waiting to see what had been stalking her.

Scott stepped through the trees. "You'll get lost if you go too far from the path," he said and tugged on her hand, trying to lead her back the way they had come.

"Go back to the party," she insisted.

"Not without you," he said.

She stopped abruptly and turned her head,

sensing something. A creature maybe, or another god that had been sent to harm her. She could feel whatever it was fix its attention on her. Her heart loped crazily in her chest. Evil vibrated in the breeze. But Scott didn't seem to feel the strange shiver in the night.

Her mind spun, trying to figure a way to get Scott to stop playing hero and go away.

"I'm meeting Brian," she lied, her heart sinking. But she had no choice. She had to get Scott to leave the woods, and quickly.

Scott let go of her hand. "He bragged that you would never get over him, but I thought he was just being Brian."

"He told the truth," Sudi said, hating the lie.

"I didn't believe the things Brian said about you," Scott answered.

Sudi wanted to hear what Brian had said and argue in her own defense, but she knew she had to hurry. She whirled around, leaving Scott alone, and ran deeper into the woods, forcing back her tears, wanting more than anything to lure the beast away from Scott and the party.

Her hands trembled, and she fumbled with

her sleeve, trying to roll it up so she could read the incantation she had written on her arm. But fear had muddled her thinking. Which spell was the right one? A pungent smell was wafting around her. She didn't know if evil had a scent, but maybe the creature coming after her did. She held up her arm and blinked back the tears distorting her vision. She had forgotten to consider how dark the night might be. Even with the milky moonlight, she could barely read the incantation.

Whatever was coming had quickened its pace.

She began to speak the spell and stopped. What if it wasn't a creature heading toward her? She couldn't just turn anyone into a dog—

She stopped in her tracks, then crept behind a vine and waited.

A mummy stepped from the foliage and paused, as if it sensed her. Its rib cage protruded where its wrapping had fallen away. Black streaks covered its dried and shrunken orange-brown skin. The eyes had fallen back into their sockets, and the lids appeared closed. Slowly, the mummy's head turned, and through slits, its gaze fell on her.

Sudi held up her arm and read the spell.

"*Goddess of magic, I entreat you, send a burning ring of your love fire around the one who beholds me. Set fire to his heart, that . . .*" She stopped. She was reading the wrong incantation.

If she were going to survive, she had no choice.

". . . *That he might love me,*" she said, finishing the incantation.

The mummy lunged toward her. Her spell had done nothing.

Sudi jerked back and slammed into the tree behind her. Pain spun up her spine. The mummy's skeletal hands grabbed her, the bony fingers pressing into her waist. Its head bent toward her with an unpleasant crack of bones, and with its closeness came a strong rancid odor.

She groaned with disgust as the mummy's face pressed against her forehead. Then, without warning, its swollen black teeth clicked against hers, and the stale taste of mold and embalming resin settled on her tongue. She pushed the mummy away. Her hands came back covered with bits of dry mummy-wrapping.

"What are you doing?" she asked, not sure the mummy understood. But she felt certain she knew: her spell had worked, after all. The mummy was trying to kiss her.

It tottered toward her again, struggling to keep its body balanced atop its stiff legs.

Sudi felt something in her mouth like a piece of broken tooth. She picked a black nugget off her tongue, then glanced at the mummy. The tip of its nose was missing. She squealed in disgust and spat.

Bile rose to the back of her throat, and she took long, slow breaths to settle her nausea.

The mummy tried to hold her in its brittle arms. Was it trying to comfort her? She ducked out of its embrace, then spat again, wishing the moldy taste would go away.

"I need to get some help," she said, rolling down her sleeves. "Stay here."

She looked into the creature's hollow eyes and

wondered if it understood. She stepped away, and when she thought the mummy was going to remain where it stood, she turned and ran wildly back to Michelle's house.

Leaves slapped her face, momentarily blinding her, but she continued on. Her heels wobbled in the mud, and her ankles twisted painfully back and forth in her unsteady shoes, but that didn't slow her pace.

When she reached the path, she paused, deciding which way to go.

Behind her, footsteps squished in the spongy soil, and then the mummy plodded between two trees, reaching out for her. Its thumbs got tangled in vines as it stumbled toward her. Its chin hit the top of her head with a terrible crack.

She choked back a scream, terrified its jaw had snapped free.

The mummy stared back at her, face intact except for the missing piece of nose. Carefully, she touched its arm. Her fingers encircled the bone. Something dry flaked off in her right palm. She prayed it was only mummy-wrapping.

"You can't come with me," she explained. "I'm

just going to get help. I promise I won't leave you out here alone."

Sudi dropped her hand and took one tentative step away.

The mummy grinned and took a wobbling step forward.

Either it was terrified of the new world in which it found itself and didn't want to be alone, or it was so in love with Sudi that it couldn't bear to be away from her. But she had to find Dalila and Meri, and she couldn't risk having the mummy trail after her.

"Okay," she said. "You can come with me, but if we hear anyone, we have to hide."

She walked with the mummy until they reached the edge of the woods, and then she peered out from behind a tree. Three girls leaned against the buffet table, dipping strawberries in chocolate, but most of the partygoers stood near the stage, snickering and mocking Michelle's performance. Sienna looked ready to run.

Maybe, Sudi thought, she could risk stepping across the lawn with the mummy; but then she saw Scott, sitting alone on the porch steps. Her chest tightened with regret. Her night of magic had deteriorated into a nightmare, and she knew intuitively that her bad dream was just beginning.

"Sudi!" Meri and Dalila called from behind her.

She turned back, surprised to see them hiking through the grass.

"We've been going up and down this path, searching for you," Meri said and displayed the scratches on her hand as proof. "Scott told us you wanted to be alone out here."

"So we knew something bad . . ." Dalila's words trailed off, and her mouth fell open as the mummy moved from the shadows and stood in the moonlight.

Meri gasped and clutched Dalila's arm. Both stood still, staring at the mummy.

"I guess you were right," Sudi admitted. "And so was Abdel. It wasn't safe for us to be out at night yet."

"But you stopped it," Dalila said, stepping closer and touching the mummy's shoulder. She flinched when its head turned.

"Gross," Meri said and took a step back. "He reeks."

"No," Dalila corrected. "Most mummies only have a musty odor. What you smell is the magic the cult used to bring his spirit back to the living world."

"Whatever," Meri said. "He still smells horrible."

"How do you know it's a he?" Sudi asked.

Both Meri and Dalila pointed in reply.

"Oh," Sudi said softly and quickly looked away.

"What spell did you use?" Dalila asked.

"That's the thing," Sudi said, hesitating. "I accidentally put a love spell on him."

She told them about the two spells and how she had used the wrong one. When she finished, Meri couldn't stop laughing, but Dalila looked worried.

"You've made a terrible mistake," Dalila said. "There's a division between the dead and the living, and those who live are not supposed to meddle with those in the underworld. The cult broke that rule, and now you have, too."

"I didn't resurrect it," Sudi argued. "The cult did."

"But what kind of love spell did you use?"

Dalila asked. "Did you bind your soul to his for all eternity? Will your spirit go with him if we find a way to send him back to his world?"

Sudi shrugged; as usual, she hadn't thought it through.

"Let's take him back to my house," Sudi said. "We'll hide him there until we can ask Abdel what to do."

"Are you sure?" Meri said. "Your parents are going to smell him."

"What else can I do?" Sudi asked. "I can't just leave him here. He probably wouldn't stay anyway. He follows me like he can't bear to be away from me."

Dalila shook her head. "The mummy's spirit was brought back, but he can't be one of the blessed dead. He must have done something evil when he was alive, or his soul would have found its way into eternal life. Do you want to take something like that into your house?"

"Especially when he's in love with you," Meri said, and playfully poked Sudi.

"Stop acting like this is a joke," Sudi said and gave Meri an angry look. "We're dealing with a demon."

"Not a demon," a dry voice corrected. "I'm a damned soul."

Sudi, Meri, and Dalila turned and stared at the mummy.

"He understands us," Sudi whispered.

CHAPTER 14

"We can't just stay here," Meri said, studying the shadows. "Other mummies could be coming."

Sudi hadn't considered the possibility that a troop of corpses might be searching for her. "How are we going to get him out of here?"

"Magic," Dalila answered mysteriously. "Wait here while Meri and I get him something to wear."

Sudi watched them leave, but she didn't think their plan to conceal him in clothing was going to work. The mummy leaned against her, his sharp elbow pressing into her, but she didn't push him away. Minutes passed, and when Dalila and Meri didn't return, Sudi began thinking about Scott again. She wiped at the corners of her eyes.

"I guess you're my date for the night," she said cynically, and gazed up at the stars. "I wish it could have been different," she started. "Why did I ever go out with Brian in the first place?"

She turned and looked at the mummy, and before she could stop, she found herself revealing her most inner thoughts and fears. She told him about Brian and Scott, telling him things she hadn't even told Sara.

He nodded sympathetically as if he understood.

Dalila and Meri returned before Sudi had even started on Michelle.

"This is the best we could do," Meri said and unfurled a black trench coat.

"We stole it off the bed where everyone had thrown their coats," Dalila explained. "But we'll return it."

Sudi was certain the coat belonged to Carter,

and she wondered if Dalila was using it as an excuse to see him again.

"People will still see the mummy's head," Meri said.

"Not if my magic works," Dalila replied. She closed her eyes and lifted her arms, with her palms up in supplication. "Queen of magic, Goddess of many names, we bow before your ruling, dear Isis, but if it pleases you, send a burning fire around this one here, and give him the flesh of his youth."

The mummy looked at them with glazed eyes, but nothing happened.

"I guess we'll have to risk walking with him after all," Meri said.

"Let's try again, together," Sudi said, and raised her palms. Meri stood next to her doing the same. They closed their eyes and repeated the incantation with Dalila.

When Sudi opened her eyes, a single red spark floated into the darkness. Other embers joined it, and soon fiery specks swirled around the mummy. Then the cinders fell to the ground, hissing, and the faint scent of charred grass wafted into the air.

Sudi blinked, adjusting her eyes to the sudden gloom. A young man, no more than eighteen, stood in the moonlight completely naked.

"Whoa," Meri said. "What happened to his mummy-wrappings?"

"They're still there," Dalila said. "This is just a disguise that will wear off quickly."

They helped the mummy into the trench coat, then guided him across the lawn.

The girls at the chocolate fountain stopped eating and stared.

"Woo-hoo!" one shouted, wiping at the chocolate on her lips. "Who's the hottie?"

"Introduce us to your friend," Lydia screamed.

"They must be high on chocolate," Sudi said. "Normally Lydia is guy shy."

"Maybe it's the mummy," Meri said, opening her cell phone. "He's really good-looking."

"Evil is always seductive," Dalila added matter-of-factly. "I'm sure that's what they're sensing."

"Great," Sudi said. "Just what all parents want their daughter to bring home."

Meri called her driver, and he was waiting at

the curb by the time they stepped into the front yard. He stared at the mummy's bare feet and ankles but said nothing.

Sudi squeezed into the back between Dalila and the mummy. Meri climbed into the front. They rode in silence, except for the mummy's frightened gasps. He winced at oncoming traffic, and twice shielded his eyes.

Finally, the sedan parked in front of Sudi's house. Dalila and Meri got out with Sudi and the mummy. They huddled near the curb.

"Maybe he should go home with me," Dalila said. "After all, my uncle is an Egyptologist and he'd probably love talking to him."

"The mummy would never stay with you," Meri said. "He'd try to find Sudi, and then he'd be lost and wandering around D.C."

"I'll get him inside," Sudi said, with a confidence she didn't feel.

They said good night, and Sudi started up the walk. She unlocked the front door as the sedan drove away and led the mummy inside.

At the base of the stairs she paused, listening. The refrigerator hummed, but that was the only sound. She gripped the banister and guided the mummy up the steps. Her heart felt ready to explode. What if her mother caught her taking this half-naked guy to her room? She'd never be able to explain this one.

She crept down the hallway past her parents' open bedroom door, feeling totally exposed. When at last she had the mummy in her room, she closed the door and slid to the floor. She didn't stand up again until her legs stopped shaking.

The mummy walked around her room, running his fingers over her dresser, and then he sprawled out on her bed.

Sudi hadn't considered how exhausted he must have felt. She unfolded the comforter and tucked it around him. "I promise I'll find a way to get you through all the gates and into eternal life."

"The beautiful west," he whispered, as if he longed for a peaceful death.

She wondered what his life had been like. In another time she might have loved him. Then a shudder ran through her. What had he done to become a damned soul?

She took a sleeping bag from the shelf in her

closet, unrolled it, crawled inside, and quickly fell asleep.

She awoke with a start. Her mother was pounding on her door. "Sudi, you're going to be late," her mother yelled. "And don't you dare cut school again. I don't want another note from your vice principal."

The mummy leaned over the edge of her bed, gazed down at her, and started to speak. Sudi struggled from her sleeping bag and placed a hand over his mouth. He kissed her palm.

"Don't say a word," she whispered. She felt his tongue on her neck. He rolled over, pulling her on top of him.

She slid off the bed and went to gather some clean underwear from her dresser.

"I have to go to school," she explained, before shutting herself in the closet and taking off her clothes. She rubbed jasmine lotion over her body, hoping it would cover the mummy's stench if it still clung to her. Then she dressed and stepped back out into the room.

The mummy stood by her window, staring out at the backyard.

"You'll have to lock the door when I leave," she said and showed him how to turn the button on the doorknob. "It's really important that no one finds you here."

He nodded and leaned over to embrace her. His lips grazed her cheek as she slipped into the hallway and closed the door behind her. She waited until the lock clicked into place, and then she ran downstairs and burst into the kitchen.

The morning news played on the TV, and the smell of burned toast filled the air. Sudi's mother stood at the sink, scraping black crumbs off her toast with a knife.

"Did you buy birdseed?" she asked when she saw Sudi.

"Yes," Sudi said, and grabbed an apple from the fruit bowl.

"Nicole and Carrie told me that they found a bird trapped in the house," her mother said. "I hope you're not trying to keep a wild bird as a pet."

"Her room smells like the inside of a chicken coop," Carrie said, and Nicole giggled.

"Very funny," Sudi said with a snide grin, but she wondered if Carrie had smelled the mummy.

"I don't want any birds close to the house," her mother continued and bit into the toast. "You've seen the mess pigeons make."

"You wouldn't poison it, would you?" Sudi asked, suddenly panicked, remembering how, as a bird, she had been unable to control the impulse to eat a beetle. "It's not like the bird did anything wrong."

"Are you all right?" her mother asked, her eyes filling with concern.

Sudi wanted to fall into her mom's arms and tell her everything.

"I'm fine," Sudi lied, and started for the door.

CHAPTER 15

Forty-five minutes later, Sudi took her assigned seat in the back of her English class. She pulled out her cell phone, flipped it open, and read a text message from Meri: *Abdel is not home.*

Sudi groaned. She couldn't keep the mummy hidden through a second night. Where had Abdel gone? Surely, he hadn't returned to Egypt. At least, she hoped he hadn't.

An odd awareness made her glance up. Her

classmates were staring at her. A few held their hands over their mouths to hide their snickering.

"Are you all right?" Carter asked, looking at her curiously. He grabbed his backpack, got up from his desk, and slid into the empty one next to her.

"Why is everyone watching me?" Sudi asked in a low voice.

"You didn't comb your hair, for one thing, and you usually wear makeup," Carter said. He scooted the desk closer to her so other students couldn't overhear. "And you smell like you were Dumpster diving. What happened?"

Normally she would have shot back with something clever, but his open and sincere manner made her pause. She reached for a snarled lock of hair and held it to her nose.

"I reek," she moaned.

"Kids are saying the breakup with Brian is affecting you," Carter explained. He placed his hand on her shoulder.

"Who said that? It's not true!" Sudi shouted, outraged. "I am not having a meltdown because of Brian. Why would I miss him? He kisses like a donkey."

Screaming laughter resounded throughout the room.

Sudi glanced at Brian, sorry for her outburst. A flicker of remorse crossed his face as if for a nanosecond he regretted the way he had treated her.

Sebastian, a guy who'd had a crush on Sudi at the beginning of the year, peered out from behind his chin-length bangs. "Sudi, how do you know what a kiss from a donkey feels like?"

Now the entire class was laughing at her.

Brian's voice boomed above the uproar. "Leave her alone," he said. "Can't you see she's losing it?"

"Get real." Sudi rolled her eyes. At least now she knew where the rumor had started. "I am not losing it!"

Carter massaged the back of her neck, trying to calm her. She pushed his hand away.

"You'll get through it," he said soothingly. "Scott's the best medicine. I told him to forget about what you did last night at the party. I mean, we all know you weren't meeting Brian, so why did you tell Scott that you were?"

Sudi shrugged.

"I figured you were still upset about the cicada thing," Carter continued. "So when he tried to kiss you—"

"He told you?" Sudi asked. The heat of a blush rose to her cheeks.

Carter nodded. "He's going to ask you out again."

"He said that?" she asked, eager to hear more.

But Mrs. Grumm walked into the room and tapped a ruler on her desk to silence the class.

"Later," Carter said and turned his attention toward the teacher.

"Good morning," Mrs. Grumm said. She pulled some papers from her carryall and set them on her desk with a sharp slap. Her glasses dangled on a chain around her neck, and her porcupine haircut made her head look too small for her barrel-shaped body.

Sudi leaned back, thinking about Scott, grateful to have almost an hour to mull over everything that was going on in her life.

"Sudi, would you like to start off by reading your essay?" Mrs. Grumm asked and sat down at her desk, biting on the tip of her acrylic fingernail.

Panic seized Sudi. She hadn't done the homework. "I haven't . . ." she stammered, trying to find an excuse, but before she could, Carter tore the title page from his work and handed it to her.

"Are you sure?" she whispered.

"It's not very good anyway," he replied. "You'll probably only get a D."

Sudi headed toward the front of the class, but when she reached the blackboard, she sensed movement near the door.

Black material, the same color as the trench coat which the mummy had worn, fluttered near the entrance. She tilted her head and craned her neck to see. Her heart raced in anticipation. The papers fell from her shaking hands.

The mummy leaned against the open door, still wearing the trench coat. But Dalila's spell had fallen away, and a withered, shrunken corpse grinned back at Sudi.

She gasped and looked at the class, hoping no one had seen him.

The tardy bell rang. The shrill sound panicked the mummy. His nails scratched the door as his hands tried to brace his body. He almost fell, then caught himself and lumbered away.

"Sudi?" Mrs. Grumm looked up and put on her glasses. "What's wrong?"

"I need to go to the nurse," Sudi said and didn't wait for permission. She bolted from the classroom and sprinted down the hallway, her footsteps banging noisily on the hard floor. She didn't see the mummy. Where had he gone? And how had he followed her to school? He couldn't just walk down the streets of D.C.

A scream echoed up the stairwell from the hallway below. Sudi charged down the steps, taking the last three in a leap.

Lydia was hurrying away from the girls' restroom, her face stricken.

"Stay out," she stammered, and tried to say more. Finally, frustrated, she waved Sudi away from the door, but she didn't stay to explain what had frightened her. She darted toward the stairs.

Sudi pushed through the swinging door and almost tripped over a fallen backpack. Lipstick, mascara, and a broken perfume bottle lay scattered on the floor. A cigarette smoldered on the dingy tiles.

The mummy stood transfixed by his reflection

in the full-length mirror. Then he saw Sudi behind him and tried to arrange his bandages.

"Why didn't you stay where I left you?" Sudi asked, approaching him carefully. If Dalila's magic had worn off, then Sudi's spell must have weakened also.

"Love made me follow you," he explained.

Sudi wondered why her magic hadn't diminished, but she didn't have time to consider the reason. She had to figure out a way to hide him.

"No wonder you spurn me," he said sadly, still gazing in the mirror. "I'm hideous."

"We need to get you away from here," she said. "That girl will come back with others, maybe even the police."

"Perhaps if you smoothed oil and perfume over my legs and arms, their beauty would return. I was strong and muscular, my legs thick and brown." He stepped closer to the mirror. "At least let me adorn my eyes. Do you have *mesd'emt* so I can paint my eyes for you?"

"We don't have time," she said.

Anxiety constricted her chest, and she had to concentrate on breathing. She didn't know how long it would be before Lydia found someone and returned. Then again, maybe it was time to let the world know about the cult and the Hour priests. But what would happen to the mummy then?

"Let's leave now," she said.

"If you could have seen me when I wore my headdress," he said. "The long hair fell thickly to my shoulders and framed my face. Queens fell in love with me once." He turned carefully and walked toward her. "Why did you bring me back?"

"I didn't," she explained. "The Cult of Anubis did and sent you to destroy me."

"That's impossible," he said. "I adore you."

"Not really," she confessed. "I cast a love spell on you, and I guess it made you forget why the cult brought you back."

She took his hand. The cold knuckle bones protruded against her palm.

"We can't let people see you," she said, leading him to the door. She peeked out.

The hallway was empty. Teachers' voices came from behind the closed classroom doors and combined in a low, dull drone.

Sudi pulled the mummy forward and guided

him to the janitor's storeroom. She opened the door, switched on the light, pulled him inside, and closed the door. The smells of ammonia and damp mops clogged the air in the small room.

"You have to stay here," she said. "No following me this time. I'm going to get a note from the nurse so I can leave school, but I'll be back."

The mummy nodded.

She opened the door and edged into the hallway, then turned and bumped into Carter. She jumped. "You scared me to death," she said. "Have you been following me?"

"Mrs. Grumm asked me to make sure you were okay," he said, a sly expression on his face.

Had he seen the mummy? Surely, if he had, he wouldn't be smirking; he'd be terrified and screaming. Still, he looked at her as if he knew her secret.

"What were you doing in the janitor's storeroom?" he asked, falling into step beside her.

"Smoking a cigarette," she lied and increased her pace, hoping he would leave her alone.

"You don't smoke," he countered.

"I do now," she said forcefully.

"Mrs. Grumm was worried about you," he

said, trailing behind her on the stairs. "You left the classroom and went the wrong way."

On the second-floor landing, Sudi stopped, and he bumped into her this time. "I told you I needed a smoke," Sudi said. "I can go to the nurse's office by myself. Go back to class, and tell Mrs. Grumm that I'm all right."

"Maybe I should stay with you," Carter said, the smug smile returning to his face.

"Go," Sudi answered and waited until he left before she continued up the next flight of stairs to the third floor.

Minutes later, with the nurse's pass in hand, Sudi returned to the janitor's closet and opened the door.

The mummy was gone.

CHAPTER 16

The sun had set, and the evening damp clung to Sudi's arms and face. She sat with Meri and Dalila behind the Lincoln Memorial and curled her toes in the wet grass, trying to ease the pain of her blisters.

"We're never going to find the mummy by walking around the District," Meri said, massaging her calves. "Maybe we should go back to Georgetown and see if Abdel's home yet."

"The mummy has probably gone back to the cult anyway," Dalila said. "If they can cast a spell strong enough to summon his spirit from death, then they must know one to make him return to them."

"Or maybe he's the lead story on the nightly news," Sudi said, trying to lighten their moods. "We haven't watched TV all day. He could be the breaking story."

She had meant to cheer her friends up. Instead, they stared back at her stone-faced. "What will happen if people discover that the dead can be brought back to life?" Dalila asked.

"I can't even imagine how gross it would be," Meri said.

Dalila shrugged. "I'd like to be able to speak to my parents again."

"But they wouldn't be like they were back then," Meri argued.

Sudi pulled on her shoes and stood. "Come on. We'd better start home."

Meri and Dalila followed her down to the walkway. They had gone only a short distance when three cabs pulled up to the curb. Tourists climbed from the first two, and then Abdel got out of the last one. His normally neat hair hung in his eyes, and his forehead glistened with sweat.

"Abdel!" Sudi shouted and ran to him, feeling an incredible surge of happiness.

Meri shrieked and hugged him.

"Where have you been?" Dalila asked, smiling.

"I've been looking for the three of you," he said, and wrapped his arms around them, squeezing tightly. "You weren't at your schools, and Dalila's uncle didn't know where she had gone off to."

"The cult sent a mummy," Sudi began, but Meri interrupted, her hands flying into the air as she excitedly continued the story. When she ran out of breath, Dalila finished for her, recounting everything else that had taken place.

Abdel nodded patiently, but he didn't seem interested in their troubles.

"If you had come to me first," he said, "I could have warned you that the mummy had only been sent to distract you from something more important."

"If a walking corpse isn't our real problem,"

Sudi said, "then I don't think I want to know what is."

Abdel looked at her. "The cult kidnapped Scott."

Sudi swallowed hard and pressed her fingers against her eyes so she wouldn't cry.

"That's against the law," Meri said. "The authorities will get involved, and I thought the cult wanted to stay low key."

"They won't hold Scott indefinitely," Abdel explained. "They'll release him quickly, but when they do, his soul will have been replaced with a demon's spirit, an evil demon."

"What should we do?" Sudi asked.

"Rescue him," Abdel said simply.

"But how?" Dalila asked. "We're not strong enough to fight the cult. They've had centuries to practice their magic, and we've only studied for three weeks."

"Besides, how are we supposed to know which spells to use?" Meri added. "We've memorized some, but they're for silly things."

Abdel seemed to find humor in their panic. "You're descended from the gods who brought order to Egypt," he said. "I have every confidence that you'll find a way, as your ancestors did when they fought the forces of chaos."

"But wait," Dalila said, clinging to his arm. "You told us that the cult wants to destroy our bloodline because once they do, no one will have the power to use the Book of Thoth to stop them."

Abdel nodded.

"So, what if this is only a trick to make us go to them?" Dalila asked.

"In every encounter, that will be a risk you'll have to take," Abdel answered.

"But what if we can't stop them?" Meri asked.

"The world will be changed," Abdel said.

"And what happens to us if we don't suc-ceed?" Sudi asked.

Abdel looked at each of them before answer-ing. "Legend says that all Descendants who fail are condemned to live with the demons in the chaos at the edge of the universe."

CHAPTER 17

Sudi closed the front door and stepped silently across the dark living room. The smell of chicken frying permeated the air, and when she neared the kitchen she could hear it crackling in the hot oil. She stood in the pantry, spying on her family.

Her mother carried a plate of steaming biscuits to the table, and her father broke into song, serenading her. His deep voice drowned out her sisters' squeals as they tried to sing along. Sudi had been part of that happiness once, but now her mind was whirring with worries that no one ever expected to face. She didn't know how to find Scott, let alone rescue him. And how did Abdel know for certain that the cult had kidnapped him, anyway? After all, he had been a druggie in California, and maybe he had taken a slide back into that lifestyle.

"Come join us." Her father sang the words to the tune of the Toreador Song from *Carmen*.

It took her a moment to realize that he was singing to her. Then she stepped into the overly warm kitchen, and sat down, wondering if this could be her last meal with her family.

"You're late," her mother said. Using a pair of tongs, she picked out a wing and a thigh from the iron skillet on the stove. She placed both on a plate and set it in front of Sudi.

"It's Monday night," Sudi said. "I thought the twins had dance class."

"We finished with this session," Nicole explained.

"We're off for two weeks," Carrie added.

"Tell us about your day," her father said as he passed her the basket of biscuits. "It must have been a good one for you to be so late." He winked.

"Things came up," Sudi said absently and stared down at her food. Normally, she loved her mother's fried chicken, but now she wondered if chickens had dreams and emotions. Did they feel the way she had when she was trapped inside a bird's body?

"If you don't want your thigh, can I have it?" Nicole asked, biting a piece of meat from her drumstick.

"Did you ever think that birds might have feelings?" Sudi asked.

Nicole looked perplexed. "Does that mean you don't want it?"

"Be a cannibal," Sudi said and pushed her plate across the table toward Nicole.

"Sudi, don't you feel well?" her father asked.

"I've become a vegetarian, all right?" Sudi replied brusquely.

Her parents exchanged a quick look, and then her mother spoke. "That's certainly all right." She passed Sudi the bowl of succotash. "Lots of people don't want their bodies to become a graveyard for animals."

"Gross!" Carrie and Nicole hollered in unison.

Sudi stared at the lima beans and kernels of corn. She couldn't eat. Nothing tasted good with tears.

"A guy told me to give this to you," Carrie said, holding up an envelope. Hieroglyphs inside a cartouche formed Sudi's name.

Sudi snapped the envelope away from Carrie. "Don't you know better than to talk to strangers?" Sudi demanded.

"What should I do?" Carrie asked snidely. "Stop answering the door because someone might bring you an invitation you don't want?"

"He came to the door?" Sudi tore at the envelope. In her haste she cut her finger on the paper's edge and cried out, then stopped and sucked the blood.

Carrie and Nicole stared at her.

Her father took the envelope and finished opening it. "It's a gift certificate to a health spa," he said. "What were you afraid it was going to be?"

Sudi shook her head. "I don't know."

Her mother took the certificate. "The Anubis Spa is elegant and pricey. Maybe you can cash in the certificate and use the money for something practical."

"It's a gift," her father said. "Let her indulge herself."

"I don't know," her mother said, absently fanning herself with the card. "The spa is connected with that cult, and I've heard some weird things about them. You know, that California touchy-feely attitude."

"It's harmless," her father said and leaned back, spreading his arms, ready to break into another song.

Sudi grabbed the invitation—she couldn't bear more happiness—and ran from the kitchen, pretending not to hear her father and mother calling her to come back.

Upstairs, she hurried into her room and closed the door, then fell on her bed and flipped open her cell phone. She had started to speed-dial Meri when someone knocked. Her father opened the door and peeked in.

"What's wrong, Sudi?" he asked and walked over to her bed. He sat down beside her. His weight made her side of the mattress lift.

"Growing pains," Sudi answered. "Things have gotten really hard lately."

"Because of Brian?" he asked.

Sudi nodded her lie.

"Sometimes young men can be heartless, because they don't know how to behave yet. They're learning to develop social skills, the same as you." Her father pulled her close to him and kissed the top of her head. "Besides, Brian is a jackass," he added. "I never liked him anyway."

Sudi pulled away from her father and walked over to her open window. "Dad, do you believe in magic?" Sudi asked.

"Of course I do," he answered.

She glanced at him, surprised.

"Today's magic is tomorrow's technology," he explained. "We use things once considered magic every day. When Marconi told his friends that he had invented a way to send messages through the air without wires, they took him to see a psychiatrist, because they didn't believe such a thing was possible. But Marconi invented the radio, and now we send pictures through the air. We all watch TV, and that's a kind of magic, so why couldn't there be more? There has to be."

Sudi leaned on the windowsill and looked out

at the starry sky. "It's scary looking up there and wondering what might be looking back at us."

"That's an odd thing to say," her father said, joining her. "Why would you feel afraid? You have me and your mom to protect you and keep you safe."

Sudi nodded, but she knew she would never feel completely safe again, because somewhere in that night sky lurked enemies: ancient gods who wanted to destroy her.

"Look," her father said excitedly. "A shooting star!"

Sudi gasped and pulled her head back inside. She eased away from the window.

"It's only a meteorite," her father said. "Your hands are trembling. Why are you so afraid?"

"A shooting star is an arrow shot by angels to stop a demon before it can reach the earth," she explained.

"Where did you learn such nonsense?" he asked and hugged her, patting her back.

"The History Channel," Sudi lied. She couldn't tell him she had read it in the Book of Thoth.

"I think we're safe from demons for tonight,"

he said and started from the room, but at the doorway he turned back, a worried expression on his face, as if the terror thrumming through Sudi had somehow telepathically transmitted to him.

"You're safe with me, Sudi," he said. "You don't need to be afraid of shooting stars or anything. If Brian . . ." He left his question unspoken, but Sudi understood.

"I'm fine," Sudi answered. "Brian never hurt me."

Her father nodded and left the room.

For the first time in her life Sudi felt ill at ease with her window open. She shut it and stared back at the black night pressing against the glass. She tugged on the cord and closed her drapes. This had to be a bad dream, some kind of cosmic joke. She couldn't be descended from the god-kings of Egypt's past. She was only a teenager who loved to dance and flirt with guys and had trouble conjugating French verbs.

But the gift certificate in her hand told her that the supernatural world was real, and that she was experiencing the ultimate reality.

Sudi stood in the Penn Quarter near Chinatown and stared across the street at the Anubis Building. Black glass covered the entire facade and reflected the fast-moving clouds. Her thoughts kept jumping forward to Scott. How were they going to find him in there? Moreover, she had thought that she would have been able to sense danger, to know instinctively that her enemy was near, but her shivering came from the cold breeze that snapped the flags and clanged the hoist clips against the towering poles behind her. That's what she told herself, anyway.

A hand touched her shoulder. She winced and spun around.

"Sorry," Meri said. The wind tossed her hair into her face. "I'm a ball of nerves, too. I almost didn't come. I kept thinking, what if it's just a spa and we do something stupid that costs my mom the nomination? She'd never, ever, forgive me."

"Then I guess you'd just have to come live with me," Sudi said, and wrapped her arm around Meri's shoulder. She felt sorry for Meri that her first worry was always about her mother's political career.

Dalila joined them. "I have the spells we'll need." She clutched a leather tube containing a papyrus from the Book of Thoth. "At least, I hope I do."

"Let's go." Sudi started across the street, dodging around traffic. She had hidden the snake wand in her baggy cargo pants, and it thumped painfully against her leg. She'd have bruises, but that was the least of her worries.

"Even if we get inside, how are we going to find Scott?" Meri asked. "The building must have ten floors."

"I guess we'll just look around," Sudi said.

"I've thought about it," Dalila said as she joined them on the curb. "I think the building covers a shaft that leads down to subterranean rooms and tunnels like the tombs in the Valley of the Kings, but instead of a burial chamber, we'll find a temple."

"That's a good start," Sudi said, and pushed through the front door, grateful that Dalila had a plan. She hurried up to the front desk.

A receptionist sat alone. She had a thin nose, large, almond-shaped eyes, and a strong resemblance to the famous bust of Nefertiti. Sudi assumed she'd probably gotten the job for that very reason.

"We don't have an appointment," Sudi said, trying to keep her voice steady. "But we were hoping we could use our gift certificates today." She slapped her card on the marble counter and immediately wished she hadn't made such a dramatic gesture.

Meri pulled a matching gift certificate from her pocket and unfolded it before handing it over. Dalila held hers between two fingers and waited for the woman to take it. They had each received an envelope the night before: a mysterious delivery from an unknown man.

The receptionist smiled, and a look of recognition crossed her face. She leafed through an appointment book too quickly; Sudi sensed that it was a meaningless show. She felt certain the woman knew what she was supposed to do.

"The only treatments available right now are for full body massages," the receptionist said.

"We'll take them," Sudi answered.

"Follow me." The woman stood and ran her hands through her glossy hair, then started down the corridor. A slit in the back of her long black dress exposed perfect legs and bare feet.

She opened a door and escorted them into a dimly lit, perfumed dressing room. Mirrors surrounded them. Sudi caught her reflection and quickly looked away. The stark fear in her eyes unnerved her; she didn't need more to add to the panicky feeling inside her.

"You can undress here," the receptionist said. She opened one of the mirrors and pointed to folded robes stacked on shelves next to bottles of lotion. "Take everything off and put these on. I'll come back in a few minutes." She left, closing the door behind her. The latch clicked into place.

"Why do they want us naked?" Meri whispered.

"That's usually the way it's done for a massage," Sudi said, pulling the wand from her cargo pants.

"It's creepy, like they're getting us ready for virgin sacrifices," Meri said and gave Sudi a meaningful glance.

"I haven't done *it* yet," said Sudi as she answered Meri's look and nervously twirled her wand like a drum major's baton. "But becoming a sacrifice to the god of chaos was never one of my fantasies for losing it."

"They probably won't kill us," Dalila said. "Just replace our souls with the spirits of dead evil-doers."

"Thanks," Meri said sarcastically. "That makes me feel a whole lot better."

"Well, it's true," Dalila answered and squeezed

the leather cylinder against her chest. "Do I have to take off all my clothes?"

"Hell, no," Sudi said. "As soon as we know the receptionist is gone, we're out of here."

Sudi pressed her ear against the door. When she didn't hear anything on the other side, she cautiously opened it and poked her head into the hallway, then slipped out. Meri and Dalila joined her, and together they stole to the end of the hallway and turned down another corridor filled with laundry carts.

"There." Meri pointed to a broad metal door. A sign on the front read: STAIRS.

Sudi hurried toward the door, pushed against the bar and stepped onto the landing. Dank, mildew-scented air engulfed her.

She waited for the door to close behind Meri and Dalila, and then she started downward.

The security lights gave little illumination, and on the next two floors they had burned out. Sudi grabbed the cold metal railing and accidentally hit the wand against the banister. The resounding clang echoed around her and made her feel as if she were descending into an endless abyss. She leaned over and peered into the shadows.

She couldn't see the bottom, and sudden terror seized her. Maybe this was a trap.

"Just continue," Dalila commanded from behind her.

Sudi started again.

A few flights later, a faint rumbling vibrated through the stairs. Sudi stopped, and Meri tumbled against her.

"Is that thunder?" Meri asked, a haunted look creeping into her eyes.

"The lord of chaos," Dalila said and paused.

The sound grew louder until a deafening roar filled the stairwell. The vibration shimmied up Sudi's legs and through her body.

"We're far below street level now," Sudi said, trying to use logic to calm her own fears. "It's probably just a Metro train passing on the other side of the wall."

The sound became muffled. Silence followed, but it was several moments before Sudi had the strength to start down again.

Finally they reached the end of stairs and faced another door. EMERGENCY EXIT was printed across the front.

"It's nothing after all," Meri said and sat on a step.

"The door probably leads out to a Metro platform," Sudi agreed, not sure if she felt disappointed or relieved that their journey had ended in nothing.

"Let's go back," Dalila said and started up the stairs, her footsteps banging noisily. "I suppose they could have hidden Scott in one of the treatment rooms."

"Or maybe he's not here at all," Meri said, gloomily. "Maybe they're holding him on a farm in Virginia. We'd better go see Abdel."

Sudi followed behind Dalila and Meri, but lost her footing on the edge of the next stair and slipped. She caught herself and glanced down. A sprinkling of sand covered the lower steps.

"Wait," she yelled, her voice echoing in the stairwell as she ran back and lunged against the door. It opened, and she stumbled over the threshold.

A blast of hot air shrieked around her, tangling her hair and lashing at her clothes. Her lungs and mouth filled with the sting of desert heat. She stepped forward, letting the door close behind her. Her wand pulsed in warning, the hieroglyphs moving in a never-ending flow.

The wind died and she found herself alone beneath a vaulted ceiling in the forecourt of an ancient temple. She lifted her head, trying to take in all the colors and gold. Paintings covered every wall.

Then, from far away, came the haunting howl of jackals, sweet sounds that awakened an odd longing, and a keen awareness that she was walking toward her death.

CHAPTER 19

Sudi turned, expecting to see the gray metal door, but the building had vanished, and in its place, golden desert stretched across the horizon, dividing an intensely blue river from a turquoise sky.

"Meri! Dalila!" Sudi shouted. The massive walls threw back her voice, and her cries echoed around her.

With a rush of wind, Meri stepped through the air, her hair whipping around her. Dalila followed after her, head bent against another gust. From behind them came the sound of an unseen door slamming shut.

Sand continued to whirl in eddies about Sudi's feet, then settled, covering the floor with swirling patterns of spiral galaxies.

Dalila rubbed her hands over the cut stone in one of the truncated pyramids that supported the pylon. Then she shielded her eyes from the sun's glare and gazed out at the desert. She inhaled sharply. "Is that the Nile?"

"Where are we?" Meri asked, looking up at the monumental gateway towering above them.

"I think we've either stepped into another dimension or we were somehow thrown back in time," Sudi answered.

"Then let's find Scott," Meri said, "and leave, before something happens to keep us here."

They stepped through the gateway and removed their jackets. Sudi took off her sweater, too, glad she had worn a short-sleeved T-shirt underneath. Then they walked between two rows of columns that looked tall enough to support the sky.

Wooden statues of Anubis guarded the next

doorway. Over that entrance, written in detailed hieroglyphs, was a warning: *only the damned enter here.*

"Should we go inside?" Dalila asked, staring at the inscription.

Sudi shrugged, not sure, and glanced at her wand. The hieroglyphs etched in the bronze lay still. She prayed that was a good sign, and started forward, pausing inside the entrance. Oil-burning lamps sat on carved wooden pillars. The flames flapped back and forth, making shadows jump and twitch. The air was stale and smelled strangely of wet copper pennies. Sudi tried to swallow, but her mouth was so dry that she coughed instead. The sudden sound of her cough reverberated down the endless corridor as if she had been leaning over a bottomless well.

The girls huddled together and slowly started down the sloping ramps and steep stairs.

"This is laid out more like a tomb than a temple," Dalila whispered as they continued downward.

The passage ended in a huge room with vivid paintings and hieroglyphs on every wall.

Sudi stared at a drawing of the solar barge passing through the underworld at night and felt a wave of nausea. Beneath the vessel, the condemned stood in fires, flames crawling around them, their mouths open in silent wails, pleading for the sun god's mercy.

"The wall paintings show the ancient Egyptian's concept of hell from the Book of the Hidden Room," Dalila explained. "My parents called the book the Amduat."

"The drawings look so real," Sudi whispered.

Meri traced her finger over the hieroglyphs below a painting of twelve men whose hearts had been ripped out and placed on the ground between their feet. "The bloody ones with torn-out hearts are welcome here," Meri translated the writing. "I bet that's not part of the original test," she added.

"I don't think this temple is a place where the blessed dead would want to find themselves," Dalila agreed.

Sudi looked away. "Let's find Scott and get out of here," she said.

But Dalila lingered, her fascination stronger than her fear.

"I remember how much paintings like these scared me when I was a little girl," Dalila reflected.

"Don't they scare you now?" Sudi didn't wait for an answer but started toward the next passageway.

"The wicked are excluded from the cycle of life," Dalila explained, "and sent to the chaos at the edge of creation."

"Where we go if we fail," Meri said solemnly.

"Maybe," Dalila continued. "Some scholars think chaos is actually in the deepest parts of the underworld. The fierce goddess Sekhmet presides over it. Her minions torture the wicked and drink their blood. But worst of all, the condemned are denied the light of the sun god." She turned slowly. "Maybe these passages lead to chaos."

"Stop!" Sudi blurted out. "Why are you going on as if this is real? These are just myths."

Meri and Dalila stared at her.

"What does it take to make you believe?" Meri argued. "Haven't we experienced enough? Do you have to have a demon dig your heart out before you'll acknowledge that this mythology is real?"

"It can't be," Sudi said; she had a strange

sensation of falling into endless space. "Please, tell me it isn't. I don't want it to be true, because if it is . . ."

"Because if it is, then everything in these paintings is what the cult wants to bring into our world," Meri said, finishing for her.

"Do you think demons will be recruited from the damned to come here and torture . . . ?" Dalila's voice faltered as if that new world were too horrifying to imagine.

Sudi forced herself to look at the paintings again. The misery she saw made her resolute. She was determined to stop the cult, but her determination wavered as a niggling little voice asked her how. She knew no incantations except for one love spell, and turning into a bird wasn't going to scare any of the creatures depicted in these scenes.

"Let's get away from here," Sudi said, marching forward.

"Wait." Meri tapped her finger on the painting of a creature with the head of a crocodile, the forelegs and body of a lion, and the hindquarters of a hippopotamus. "Dalila, is this the creature you become when you transform?"

"For now, anyway, I look like Ammut," Dalila said unhappily. "She lives in the underworld and devours the hearts of the wicked."

"We'd better hurry," Sudi said and hit her wand twice on the floor before starting forward again.

Meri and Dalila followed her this time, and together they continued on until a larger corridor crossed the hallway in which they stood. Sudi headed toward an entrance cut in the rear wall, but paused, as she became aware of faint singing.

Suddenly, Dalila grabbed her arm, and hurried her behind a massive pillar. Meri fell against her, her teeth chattering with fear.

Sudi peered out.

A man marched toward them, carrying a pole; a headless black animal pelt that looked like that of a dog hung from the top like a flag. Behind him, a priest wearing a cloak made from leopard skins walked solemnly, carrying a golden bowl in the crook of his arm. His head was shaved, and thick kohl rimmed his eyes. On his chest he wore a pectoral ornament of a vulture, and several amulets.

Sudi recognized the ankh, the T-shaped cross

with the loop handle. It was a symbol of life and divine immortality. A gold cylindrical tube clicked against the other charms; she wondered what it held inside.

The priest dipped his fingers into the small bowl and sprinkled water over the ground and pillars, ritually cleansing the path to the sanctuary.

A drop hit Sudi's forehead. The water burned, scalding her skin.

Meri slapped her hand over Sudi's mouth and held her tightly to keep her from crying out. Sudi felt defiled and, using the tail of her T-shirt, she frantically wiped at the water. Finally, she was able to peek out again and watch, through tear-blurred vision.

A procession of men and women dressed in white followed the priest into another room. The people looked ordinary; they could have been Sudi's neighbors or classmates. Nothing about them appeared particularly evil. Sudi continued watching, and then at the end of the line, she saw the three girls from her drama club who skulked about the hallways at Lincoln High. Dressed in transparent linen gowns, they danced with sinuous grace, so unlike the shyness they showed at school. Sudi wondered if the cult leaders had deceived them, or did they know they were devoting their lives to bringing chaos to the world? Sudi felt guilty that she hadn't done more to defend the girls when other kids made fun of them. Maybe one word of kindness could have made a difference in their lives.

The three girls spun across the threshold, singing. Then the voices of all the worshippers rose, and the din of rattles, drums, and clappers joined the revelry.

Sudi motioned for Dalila and Meri to follow her. She sprinted across the corridor and snuck inside the sanctuary, easing along the back wall behind a line of pillars. She hid in a dark alcove behind a row of reclining jackals, her heartbeat thudding in her ears. Meri and Dalila squeezed beside her, trying to control their nervous breathing.

The priest in the leopard skin waited in front of a pair of ornate gilded doors.

Two other men, completely shaven of all body hair and wearing low-slung white kilts with pleated front panels, took embers from a stone cauldron and lit incense. As the smoke curled into the room, the two men stepped to either side of the shrine. When the priest nodded, they opened the doors, revealing the statue of a man with an animal's head that resembled an anteater's, with tall, square ears.

The worshippers fell to their knees, but the priest remained standing, gazing up at a statue of his god Seth. A strange aura emanated from the towering image, and soon the air became dense and cold, frosting the pillars and floor with odd patches of ice.

"That's unusual," Dalila whispered. "Only the pharaoh was allowed to stand before a god."

"Maybe the priest is descended from the first pharaohs, like we are," Meri answered in a low voice.

Silence filled the room; the worshippers anticipated something momentous.

Then the priest spoke. *"Du ut des."*

The congregation repeated the words.

"What does that mean?" Sudi whispered.

"'I give in order that you give,'" Dalila replied softly. "They want something from Seth."

"Father of Anubis," the priest said, lifting a vessel in his hands. "We give you this offering."

He poured water from a *heset* jar over a long object covered with a white cloth that lay on top of a wooden funerary couch.

Sudi set her wand down. Then, holding on to the snout of one of the jackal statues for balance, she pulled herself up onto the tips of her toes to see.

Scott lay on the table in front of the priest, apparently unconscious.

Terrified, Sudi ducked back down behind the pillar.

"It's Scott," she whispered. "What will we do if they start to sacrifice him?"

Dalila opened her mouth to speak, but the priest's deep voice interrupted her.

"God of violence, chaos, and storm," the priest said, and the vaulted ceiling amplified his invocation. His words resonated and seemed to come from all directions. "Spirit of anger and rage, bring forth the Descendants of Horus who block our way."

"That's us," Meri whispered, pressing closer to the floor.

Dalila looked as if she were going to faint. "Do they know we're here?"

"I don't think so," Sudi answered, and climbed back on the jackal statue, her feet resting on its forepaws. She strained her neck, trying to see what the priest was doing to Scott.

Thunder shook the walls, and the boom resounded through Sudi. Her hands slipped, and she lost her balance. She fell into one of the patches of slick ice and skidded across the floor.

The congregants turned and gazed down at her, their eyes fierce with hate, and then they broke into jubilant song and prayer.

CHAPTER 20

Thunder shook the room, and the pillars holding the oil lamps rocked uneasily. Flames sparked and spit red embers into the air. The two lower-ranked priests who had opened the shrine walked Dalila, Meri, and Sudi to the front of the sanctuary.

"I'm sorry," Sudi said, even though she doubted that her friends could hear her over the uproar. She had been too reckless; it was her fault that they were all going to be sent to live with the demons in chaos.

They stopped in front of the high priest.

"You two could have done better without me," Sudi said to Meri and Dalila. "You'd probably have already rescued Scott."

"All the votes aren't in yet," Meri answered. "It's not time to give a concession speech."

Sudi nodded, but she didn't know how Meri could remain optimistic.

"We still have the Book of Thoth," Dalila added and faced the congregation, holding her back straight. "I left the leather pouch behind the pillar. The priests didn't know what was inside it, so if we can get back to it, we can still find an incantation to stop them."

Sudi nodded, but she didn't feel confident.

The two lesser priests lifted the funeral couch and carried Scott across the sanctuary. They set him down in front of the line of jackal statues.

"They're not going to sacrifice Scott," Sudi whispered.

"Not when they have the three of us," Meri answered.

Before Sudi could apologize again, the high priest held up his hand and the room became silent.

"Bring Sankhkara forward," the priest ordered,

watching Sudi closely. "Let's see if your love spell is stronger than the power of Seth."

The congregants shuffled, opening a path that led to an upright coffin on the opposite side of the room. The image of a man was sculpted on the gold front. The two lesser priests unfastened the lid. The mummy stood inside, now wearing a headpiece and jewelry made of lapis lazuli.

Sudi wondered how the mummy had traveled from Lincoln High without becoming breaking news on Channel 7. Someone in the congregation must have helped him. For no reason that she understood, she thought of Carter. He couldn't be one of them, but she searched the crowd for him anyway and felt a sense of relief when she didn't see him. But then she caught another familiar face. She looked again, uncertain. Had she seen Brian? Was he part of the cult? Her stomach knotted. Maybe that was her strange connection to him.

The mummy lurched forward, his arms crossed over his chest. Slowly, he brought his hands down to his sides. People stepped back when the mummy passed them as if they were anxious about their safety.

"Sankhkara died on his sixteenth birthday," the priest said to Sudi. "A strong soul, but too trusting. We used his kindness to deceive him. He had a proper burial, but we desecrated his tomb and made it impossible for him to pass through all the gates and join the blessed dead; he no longer had the Book of Gates to guide him because we covered it and replaced it with spells of our own. Now we use his corpse to kill."

Sankhkara stopped in front of the priest.

"Destroy the three," the priest ordered. "Start with the one you love."

The congregants eased back as if they had witnessed Sankhkara's brutality before.

Sankhkara shifted his weight, turning clumsily, and through thin slits, his death-frosted eyes found Sudi.

She cringed and backed up. Her throat tightened around a scream. The mummy had been sent to the party to end Sudi's life, but she had never considered how he had planned to do it. Even now she couldn't imagine what his brittle body could do, but she also knew she didn't want to find out.

He took slow, awkward steps toward her and stopped, his face inches from her own.

Meri and Dalila squeezed closer, wrapping their arms around Sudi's waist.

"He'll have to take all three of us together," Meri said, pressing her cheek against Sudi's shoulder.

Sankhkara raised his arm.

Dalila cried out and buried her face against Sudi.

"I'm so sorry," Sudi said, and tried to remember the spell she had cast on him before. Maybe if she could make him fall in love with her again she could stop him. But her mind spun, and the incantation that came forth was a jumble.

"Send a circle of fire around this one here," she said and stopped. It was useless to try. She closed her eyes and waited for the attack.

The priest laughed, enjoying her failure.

"Beware the priest," Sankhkara whispered. "He's a spirit who feeds upon weak and helpless souls. I'll protect you as best I can."

Sudi's eyes flashed open.

"He's not going to kill you," Meri said.

"Your love spell is stronger than the priest's command," Dalila added.

Sudi glanced at the priest and caught a flicker of rage before his expression turned coldly confident again.

"Why wasn't the priest able to remove my spell?" Sudi asked in a hushed voice.

"Our magic must be far stronger than we think," Dalila answered.

"Great," Sudi said. "Now all we have to do is figure out how to use it."

The priest grabbed Sankhkara's arm and pulled him back. "So, her love spell is stronger than your fear of the second death?"

"What is the second death?" Sudi asked Dalila.

"His soul will be damned," the priest answered before Dalila could speak, "and he'll forever be excluded from the cycle of life."

"You can throw my body to the dogs," Sankhkara responded defiantly. "I'll gladly suffer the fate of the damned. It was worth knowing the love I felt when I looked into her eyes again."

"Again?" Sudi asked. "What do you mean, again?"

But no one answered her.

The priest raised his hands to the statue of Seth.

"Lord of chaos, who brought death into the world," the priest intoned. "We give you the three Descendants and the son of the pharaoh Mentuhotep."

A crash of thunder startled Sudi. The boom reverberated through the sanctuary. The floor shook, and the vibrations quivered up her spine. Cracks shot across the ceiling. Tiny veins ran down the walls. Chunks of plaster fell, and dust clouded the air.

"Seth is going to kill us," Sudi said. "And I don't think he cares how many of his worshippers he takes with us."

"Why should he?" Dalila answered. "He's been trying to end the bloodline of Horus since practically the beginning of time."

Meri pinched Sudi's arm. "Carpe diem."

"Is that a spell?" Sudi asked.

"It's Latin for 'seize the day,'" Meri answered. "Mom uses it whenever she has an opportunity."

Then Sudi saw the reason Meri looked so

happy. Most of the worshippers were staring up at the statue, their faces filled with awe. Others had fallen to the floor, bowing with their eyes closed. A few had hidden their faces in their hands. No one was watching Sudi, Meri, and Dalila.

"Go," Sankhkara ordered and trundled forward, determined to protect them from anyone who tried to stop them.

The girls ran back to the pillar and hid behind it.

Dalila grabbed the leather case and pulled out the scroll.

"Do something while I find the right incantation," Dalila said.

"Like what?" Sudi asked.

"I don't know," Dalila answered. "Try anything." Her fingers fumbled with the scroll, her hands trembling so violently she couldn't open it. She lost her grip, and the papyrus fell. It rolled across the floor away from her.

Dalila started after it as thunder exploded and rumbled through the sanctuary. She lost her balance and pitched backward, slamming into the wall.

Three fire lamps tumbled from their pilasters.

Pottery smashed, and flames raced across the spilled oil toward the scroll.

"No!" Dalila shouted.

Sudi dove after the papyrus. She landed on her belly and skidded toward the flames. The fire reached the scroll first. Flames licked the edges, and smoke curled around the ancient writing.

Sudi tried to grab it, but the blaze shot higher, scorching her. She jerked her hand back and licked the blisters, then reached out again and clutched the scroll. Flames hissed and shot after her. She scooted back.

Meri slid next to her, and together they beat out the fire on the papyrus.

The worshippers watched. Some edged closer.

The papyrus was still smoldering when Sudi handed it back to Dalila.

"We don't have time to look for an incantation," Dalila said, her eyes fixed on the congregants.

The two lesser priests circled around them, crowding nearer.

"Seize them," the high priest ordered, but the lesser priests remained wary. And then Sudi saw the reason for their hesitation. Sankhkara guarded the front of the pillar, bravely ignoring the flames.

Sudi pulled Meri and Dalila behind the pillar again. Smoke stung her eyes, and she coughed as the fires continued to burn toward them.

"Maybe if we used our other powers," Dalila said, holding her hands over her mouth and nose to filter the smoke.

"You mean, change into a bird?" Sudi asked over another roll of thunder. "What good would that do?

"A cat's not going to help," Meri said. "But a cobra could scare them."

Sudi and Meri stared at Dalila.

"I can't," she answered.

"It's our only chance," Sudi said. "Your poison could kill one of them, and maybe that would frighten the rest away."

Dalila turned pale, and Sudi understood. Dalila would never be able to transform into a cobra and strike, because hurting someone was against her gentle nature.

"You don't have to bite anyone," Sudi said. "Just spread your hood and hiss. Maybe that will be enough."

"If we don't do something, they're going to kill us," Meri added.

"I haven't been able to change into a snake," Dalila said. "I become that monster Ammut."

"Just try," Sudi coaxed and held on to the pillar as another thunderclap ruptured the air and made the floor sway.

Dalila closed her eyes and began reciting her incantation. Her face convulsed, and then her lips and chin stretched into a long, tapering jaw with jagged, dangerous teeth. The thick, armorlike skin of a crocodile began to cover her cheeks and snout. Her mouth snapped hungrily.

Sudi and Meri jumped back.

"Maybe we didn't think this through," Sudi said.

Tawny-colored fur spread over Dalila's arms. Her hands turned into paws with sharp, curved claws. Hair grew, circling her reptilian face with a lion's mane.

Finally, her legs bent and shrank into stumps, and within seconds her back end looked like the rear of a hippopotamus. Her short, thick tail twitched. She roared and waddled through the fire out into the congregation.

"It's Ammut!" someone yelled.

"They've conjured the devourer of hearts!" another voice shouted.

Screams became louder than the thunder.

The priest's panicked voice shouted over the cries. "Seth will protect you."

Sudi peeked out and watched the congregants. Their fear of Ammut seemed stronger than their belief in Seth. They pushed and shoved, trying to escape Dalila, but the fires blocked their way. They slammed into each other and stampeded past the statue of Seth in an attempt to reach the exit without running through the flames.

The giant statue swayed.

The priest ran to it and braced his hands against the legs to stop its fall, but the image toppled anyway. Granite splintered. The impact hurled dagger-size chunks of stone around the room.

Sudi ducked as a slab hit the pillar and made it wobble.

The shrieks and wails from worshippers continued to rise, and then the last congregant limped from the room. The panicked voices and running footsteps faded. Quiet returned. The crackling fires were the only sound left in the room.

Dalila transformed back into a girl and couldn't stop grinning. "They think we conjured Ammut," she said. "They were afraid I was going to eat their hearts as punishment for their wicked lives."

"You should have seen yourself," Meri said, and placed a hand over her mouth trying to stop her giggles. "Your butt was humongous."

"We'd better get Scott and leave," Sudi said, "before someone decides to come back."

"I think they'll be too afraid to return," Dalila said, surveying the broken granite. "The statue was Seth's visible body on earth. He'll demand retribution for destroying his image."

A clatter made Sudi turn. Rocks tumbled from a pile of rubble. The high priest pulled himself up and wiped at the blood trickling down his face. His attention focused on Sudi.

"I will appease the lord of chaos," he said as a black aura grew around him.

At first Sudi thought it was only the smoke from the fires, but the nimbus around the priest continued to grow, churning wildly. Demonic shapes formed and darted from the cloud as if eager to attack, only to roll back as other, crueler faces swelled and retreated. The stench of tombs and death saturated the air.

"What is it?" Meri asked, her fingers cold in Sudi's hand.

"I don't know," Dalila answered, pulling Sudi and Meri backward behind a line of flames.

The priest curled his fingers and gathered the spectral streams into a ball. He flung the sphere at Sudi. The orb screeched toward her, and the sanctuary filled with the cries from a horde of demons.

CHAPTER 21

The thick blackness spun toward Sudi. The demons imprisoned within it squirmed and thrashed, writhing over and around each other, trying to be the first to attack. She stood defenseless, watching death hurtling toward her, and forgot to breathe. She had failed her parents, her sisters, and her friends, but mostly she had failed herself.

Sankhkara lurched forward and threw himself between Sudi and the sphere. He held her against his hollow chest. The globe hit his back and disappeared inside him. His mouth opened in a grimace, and he collapsed.

Sudi fell to her knees beside Sankhkara. How many people had to suffer because she had screwed up?

"I think he's dying," Sudi cried out.

"He's already dead," Meri answered, kneeling next to Sudi.

"The demons will take his soul to chaos unless we can cast our spell quickly," Dalila explained, joining them.

"Where's the incantation to send him back to be with the blessed dead?" Sudi asked, turning to Dalila.

"I'll get it," Meri said and raced back to the pillar where they had left the papyrus.

"You can't save him," the priest said as the black vapors began pulsing around him again.

Sankhkara lifted his skeletal hand and touched Sudi's cheek. "It was worth it to save you," he said, and then he began to pray. "Creator, maker, giver of breath, Amon, the one supreme deity."

"That won't help," the priest taunted.

"We'll save him," Sudi countered, and when she looked up, she noticed the priest's amulets.

"The ankh," Sudi whispered to Dalila. "It's a symbol of life. Would it help?"

"It might keep Sankhkara's spirit here long enough for us to recite the spell," Dalila answered in a soft voice.

Without thinking, Sudi leaped up and lunged past Sankhkara. She threw herself forward and tackled the priest. His aura curled around her as she fell on top of him. They skidded together over the jagged pieces of broken granite.

Sharp fragments cut Sudi's fingers, and warm blood trickled down her thumb as she clutched the priest's ankh and yanked hard. The shadows surrounding him gathered hungrily around her face, slipping into her mouth and leaving a vile taste. She choked, feeling her breath being sucked away, but that didn't stop her. She pulled again, and this time the chains broke.

Gold charms bounced and clanked across the floor, but the ankh remained in her palm. The priest tried to wrestle the talisman from her. A black line shot from his aura and encircled her arm, squeezing it until her fingers felt numb.

Then, unexpectedly, the shadow dropped its hold, and a groan gurgled from the priest's lips. The black nimbus retreated inside him.

Sudi rubbed her wrist. "The ankh must have been keeping him alive," she said. With renewed hope, she placed the ankh on Sankhkara's chest as Meri joined them and unfurled the scroll.

"You have to remove the love spell you put on him," Dalila said, "in case it interferes with the one to send his soul to rest."

Meri handed Sudi the blackened papyrus, opened to the proper spell.

In the smoky light, Sudi read the hieroglyphs: *"Goddess of magic, I entreat you, remove your love fire from around the one who beholds me. Extinguish the love in his heart, that he and I might be free from desire."*

She handed the papyrus back, and, as Meri and Dalila began reciting the other spell, she leaned over Sankhkara again and held his bony hand.

"You didn't need magic to make me love you," Sankhkara confessed. "Our souls have been one since the beginning of time, but fate has cruelly separated us."

Then a thin vapor escaped his lips and spread into a golden mist above them before vanishing.

"Let's get Scott," Meri said. She hurried over to where Scott lay.

Sudi wiped her tears and stood slowly. The depth of her sadness surprised her. She walked behind the pillar and found her wand. On her way back, she picked up the golden tube that the priest had worn around his neck and stuck it in her pocket.

"Wake up," Meri said, nudging Scott. "It's time to go home."

Scott sat up and looked around. The white linen that had covered him dropped to the floor.

"He's naked," Meri squealed, and stared brazenly.

Dalila turned her back. "Cover up," she ordered.

Sudi wanted to look, but kept her gaze focused on Meri instead.

"The spa lost your clothes," Meri said with a mischievous grin. "Can you believe that? So you'll have to wear the sheet home."

"Spa?" Scott looked befuddled. He pressed his

fingers against his eyes. "What am I doing in a spa?"

"You got hurt playing rugby," Sudi said as Meri wrapped the linen around his waist. "Your coach thought a massage and a soak in a whirlpool might help."

"I don't remember," Scott said and looked around the room.

"Maybe you have a concussion, then," Dalila said with convincing authority.

"Then why didn't they take me to the hospital?" he asked as he hobbled forward. His bare foot kicked a piece of granite. "What is all this mess?"

"They're remodeling," Sudi answered.

Sudi and Meri pulled Scott into the next corridor. He walked sluggishly, his breathing labored. He kept wiping his eyes, as if his vision were blurred.

"Do you think he's all right?" Sudi asked.

"He's in a daze," Meri whispered. "He's probably wondering if he's been doing drugs again."

Finally they reached the massive gateway that led out to the desert sand. Scott leaned against the wall, shaking his head, still trying to awaken from a bad dream.

Meri stopped. "How do we get back?" she asked. "The door is gone."

The sun rested on the horizon, its heat warming Sudi's face. Even so, she stepped forward, certain the scenery was a sham. She closed her eyes so her vision couldn't deceive her. Then, leading with her hands, she continued until her fingers touched something solid. She smoothed her palms across the cold metal and found a protruding doorknob. She turned it. A latch clicked, and she started to open the door.

Without warning, the still air became filled with violently rotating winds. Gusts shrieked around her and fought to close the door. Her hair whipped into her eyes. Her fingers loosened their hold, and the metal began slipping from her grasp.

She refused to fail her friends this time. Strength rose inside her.

"Hurry!" she yelled, and used her foot to brace the bottom edge of the door.

Meri and Dalila rushed through, pulling Scott with them. The windstorm caught the cloth wrapped around him. The tail end flapped out and snapped against Sudi's cheek.

Sudi grappled with the door, trying to pull herself inside, but the gusts were stronger, and she was losing the struggle. Sand whirled about her, scraping her cheeks and clogging her nose. She couldn't breathe or open her eyes. She hadn't escaped her fate after all. She sensed intuitively that when the door blew shut, she would never be able to open it again.

CHAPTER 22

A sudden, violent gust hit the door, and it started to close. Sudi tightened her grip. Her chest heaved, her lungs struggling to get air, but she only sucked more sand into her mouth and nose. She coughed and spit, then stopped. Something moved within the swirling sand. A dark shape was coming toward her. She squinted, protecting her eyes, and tried to see what was in the storm with her, but before she could make out the profile, warm fingers wrapped around her wrist. Other hands pushed against the door, opening it.

Meri and Dalila pulled her inside the stairwell.

Sudi tripped forward, gasping, and collided with her friends. The door slammed behind them, and then all four lost their balance and tumbled to the floor. Sudi rested her cheek on the cold concrete, and took in deep gulps of the dank air, the odor of mildew replacing the smell of dry desert sand.

"To us!" Meri shouted, jumping up. "We did it."

Dalila clapped and pulled Sudi to her feet. "All of us got out."

Sudi laughed and gave her friends a bear hug. "We survived."

"All right," a deep voice came from the steps overhead. Scott stared down at them. "Enough with the lovefest. Let's get out of here."

"We're coming," Dalila shouted excitedly, and ran up the stairs.

Sudi brushed sand from her clothes and hair and used the tail of her T-shirt to wipe her eyes. When she finished, she studied the door. "Do you think that other place is still there?" she asked Meri.

"You don't really want to see, do you?" Meri asked.

"Maybe," Sudi answered. Her curiosity was becoming greater than her fear. She placed her hand on the doorknob.

"Don't!" Dalila yelled, hanging over the railing.

Sudi opened the door anyway. She and Meri stared out at the Metro platform. The dim lights gave the vast room a gloomy feeling. A train sped by, and from its passage a current of warm air rushed over them.

"The desert vanished," Meri whispered. "How did it just disappear?"

"I don't know," Sudi replied and let the door close. "Scott's right. Let's get out of here."

Meri and Sudi ran up the stairs and hurried after Dalila and Scott. Together, they walked through the spa. No one tried to stop them. An attendant glanced up but didn't even ask if they were lost.

At the front door, Sudi caught a glimpse of herself in a mirror and paused as the others rushed outside. She was encrusted with sand, her hair a tangle. She had lost one shoe and had no recollection of when that had happened.

As she started to leave, an odd sensation made her turn. The high priest stood behind her. The kohl liner no longer circled his eyes, but he was definitely the same man, and somehow alive again. He wore an Armani suit, with a gold ankh hanging over his black sweater. He leaned against a sign posted in the entrance that announced the opening of a new teen club called The Jackal.

"I hope you'll return soon," he said. "I'll leave VIP passes for you and your friends at the front door of my club. I think you'll like the atmosphere."

Sudi pointed the tip of her wand at him and smiled back. "You bet," she said, and twirled the rod dangerously close to his face. "I've got a feeling we'll be seeing a lot of each other."

She turned and ran outside without listening to his reply.

Meri and Dalila were waiting for her in a black sedan that was parked near the entrance. Scott sat between them in the backseat.

"Get in," Meri said. "We'll take you home."

"No," Sudi said. "I want to walk."

"Like that?" Meri asked.

Sudi nodded.

"Be careful," Dalila whispered.

"I have to go to one of those functions with Mom," Meri said, "but I'll call you as soon as I get home." Then she spoke to her driver and the sedan pulled away.

The sun had set by the time Sudi reached her house, and she was shivering from the cold. She had left her jacket and sweater in that other dimension, somewhere in ancient Egypt. She stepped inside and called out a hello, grateful to be home. When no one answered, she assumed that her parents had already left for the Kennedy Center. Her sisters were spending the night with their best friend, Elena.

In the kitchen, she drank two glasses of water and then opened the cylindrical charm that the priest had worn. She pulled out the tiny piece of papyrus rolled inside and read an oath from Seth that cursed anyone who harmed the priest.

Sudi stuck both back in her pocket, then

picked up her wand and started up the stairs. She was too exhausted to worry about curses tonight. She was going to shower, do her nails, and then find a party; she was never too tired for fun.

As she stepped into her room, a cold draft blew over her. Her window was open, the drapes askew, one panel torn from the rod. Her muscles tensed and, as she started to turn, someone grabbed her around the waist.

CHAPTER 23

Sudi dropped her wand and wrestled against the arms restraining her. She bit her attacker's hand.

"Ouch!" her assailant screamed as he let go.

She turned, ready to kick.

Scott stood behind her, head bent, studying the tooth marks on the fleshy mound of his thumb.

"You're lethal," he said, looking down at her.

"Scott?" Sudi asked. "Were you trying to scare me to death?" Before he could answer, a more important question came to her. "Why did you break into my room?"

"Something crazy happened today," he said, stepping closer. He ran his finger over her cheek and then held up the tip of his finger to show her the sand. "I don't know what it was exactly, but I called my coach and he never sent me for a massage, and if that place was a spa it was a really weird one. I have this odd feeling you rescued me."

She glanced back at her torn drapes. "Next time you have a question, do you think you could just call me?"

"Did you save me from something, Sudi?" he asked, his fingers brushing through her hair. Sand spilled onto her shoulders.

She tried to find the words to explain what had happened but only nodded instead. Maybe memories were coming back to him, and if so, what was she going to say?

"You still owe me a kiss," he said and leaned down, his lips hovering inches from hers. "I've waited a long time," he murmured and waited for her permission.

"Me, too," she agreed. He touched her. She

had never felt a kiss as good as his, and when he pulled back, a sigh escaped her lips. Her hands slipped under his T-shirt, her fingers spreading up over his chest. Touching him stirred a longing in her; she wanted more than his kiss. She became suddenly aware that her parents and sisters weren't home, and that her bed was only a few inches away.

He smiled down at her, obviously understanding her thoughts, and gently pulled her toward her bed.

"I like you, Scott," she whispered. "But I'm not ready."

"Ready for what?" he teased and sat on the edge of her bed. He pulled her down until she was sitting on his knee.

"I need a shower and—"

He pressed a finger over her mouth to silence her. "You look beautiful to me."

Doubt shimmered through her as he held her tightly, his lips trailing up the side of her neck. His kisses were muddling her thinking, and his behavior didn't seem like Scott's. Why had he broken into her house? And she didn't like the way he was pressuring her now.

A sudden, frightening thought came to her. She and her friends had rescued Scott, but they hadn't bothered to find out whether a demon had already taken possession of Scott's body. Adrenaline raced through her. Scott should have been stunned to find himself inside an Egyptian temple, but he hadn't been. He had barely asked any questions. With rising panic, she realized that a demon from chaos wouldn't have been surprised.

She pushed herself off his knee and picked up her wand. The hieroglyphs moved from top to bottom, warning her that a demon was approaching. She pointed the snake head at Scott, but he only chuckled, low in his throat. She didn't know how to use the magic, but she had another sport in mind. Her hands trembled as she gripped the wand like a baseball bat, ready to strike a home run. But if she killed the demon with her swing, wouldn't she kill Scott as well? And what if Scott wasn't possessed at all, and breaking through her window was his idea of romance?

"What are you doing?" Scott asked, a puzzled look on his face.

Sudi hesitated too long.

Scott seized the wand and tossed it across the room. It hit the wall with a loud clank.

"How did you figure it out?" he asked, clenching her in a tight hold. The gentleness was gone from his touch; the pressure from his fingers caused her shoulder to throb.

An eerie sound at the open window made Scott turn. Patty Pie arched his back and hissed, his front paw clawing at the air.

Scott chuckled and eased his grip as Pie leaped onto an overhanging branch and ran away.

The interruption was all Sudi needed. She pulled free and ran across the room, with Scott close behind her. She opened the door and spun to the other side, then pushed hard, hitting Scott with the door's edge. He yelled and held his face, staggering. Blood trickled from his nose.

She raced down the stairs, two at a time, and ran out into the night. The porches of the row houses extended out onto the sidewalk like an obstacle course. She dodged one iron railing, only to find herself rushing into the next barrier of stairs. Even so, she tried to stay close to the buildings and under the trees, hoping their shadows would conceal her.

Lights came on in the surrounding houses, and behind her, a door opened. But she did not turn back. The safety within the homes was an illusion, and she knew that if she went inside, instead of finding sanctuary, she would only bring death to the families who lived there. And then, what would happen to Scott if the demon decided to leave him after it had massacred a dozen people? He'd end up in jail for life at best.

Sudi quickened her pace, knowing she had to fight the demon on her own.

By the time she reached the canal, her side ached and her legs burned. She couldn't run any farther, even though she could hear Scott's feet pounding on the hard dirt. She crouched under a bush where no one could see her transform.

Then she raised her hand to the night. "Amun-Re, eldest of the gods in the eastern sky, mysterious power of wind, make a path for me to change my earthly *khat* into that of beloved Bennu."

Immediately, her skin prickled. Feathers grew from her fingers as her arms contracted and her bones popped. Then, with her monocular vision, she saw Scott. He had found her after all. She scurried from beneath the branches and took long strides, flapping her wings before her transformation was even complete. Wind rushed around her, holding her wings, and she lifted off the ground.

Scott screamed and jumped. He grabbed her bird-claw. Pain shot through her, and she spiraled down. She hit the ground, transforming back into a girl, and skidded across moldy leaves. Her back ached, and she thought for sure her leg was broken.

"Now," Scott snickered. Fire burned in his eyes.

Sudi fought against the dizziness and tried to remember a spell that could help her. Her mind jumped from one hieroglyphic script to the next, but each time, she came up with useless incantations. Casting a spell for glossy hair was not going to stop the demon who stood over her.

CHAPTER 24

At first, Sudi thought the murmuring came from the quiet flow of water, lapping against the canal banks, but slowly she realized the soft sounds were whispers, coming from the shadows. She struggled against the pain to rise up on her elbow and listened intently, trying to understand what the hushed voices were saying.

Scott looked up, wary, and stepped into the darkness beneath the trees. He growled, low in his throat, a feral sound, as if warning others away.

Maybe a pack of demons had come to steal her from him. She imagined the creatures pouncing and snarling as they tore her apart.

Then, without warning, a cat sprang from the branches above Scott and landed on his back, its claws ripping into his shirt.

He cried out and flung his hands, trying to knock the cat away.

The feline yowled, an unnatural, half-human shriek. Its sleek black fur sparkled with glitter, an earring dangled from its ear, and a velvet scrunchie slipped from its head. Already its hind legs were turning back into those of a girl wearing spiky red heels.

In the same moment, Dalila crouched beside Sudi. "We have to draw hieroglyphs on Scott's chest," she said breathlessly, "to make the demon's spirit leave him."

Sudi looked at her, surprised. "How did you know I was in trouble?"

"Your cat, Pie, told Meri's cat, Miwsher," Dalila explained.

"The feline underground," Sudi said, and pulled herself up onto her knees, ignoring the jabbing pain.

Scott bellowed and spun around. Meri fell to the ground, transforming back into a girl. Her black dress, cut low in the back, was torn and rumpled, her party makeup smeared. But her skin still glistened with golden glitter.

Dalila and Sudi scrambled to her, each grabbing an arm, and drew her back, away from Scott.

He stood in the dim light, grumbling and baring his teeth in an ugly grimace.

Sudi stared back at her enemy, feeling a queasy dizziness. "What if we can't get the demon to leave Scott? Do we have to—" she stopped. She couldn't say the words.

"Kill him?" Dalila finished for her.

"Don't even think about that," Meri ordered.

Scott retreated into the shadows.

"What now?" Sudi asked. Darkness surrounded them; Scott was probably sneaking about, planning a surprise attack from another angle.

"I'll find him," Meri answered. Her eyes

changed back into those of a cat. "There," she whispered. "He's next to the maple tree."

"Do you think we can really restrain him long enough to write something on his chest?" Sudi asked, feeling doubtful.

"You bet." Meri kicked off her shoes, reached up under her dress, and rolled off her panty hose.

"What are you doing?" Dalila asked, her frightened eyes searching the shadows for Scott.

"We need ropes," Meri replied as she stretched out the legs of the panty hose. "We'll tie his wrists behind his back."

"How can you be so sure?" Sudi asked. She couldn't even see Scott in the gloomy depths.

"Jeez, haven't you ever heard of positive thinking?" Meri said. She didn't wait for an answer. "We charge him on the count of three. One. Two. Three!"

Sudi ran blindly, following Meri's lead. Suddenly, Scott stood in front of her. She screamed and lunged into him. He stumbled backward, tripping over his own feet. His back hit the tree.

Meri grabbed one wrist, Dalila the other, and

before Scott could react, they were tying the ends of the panty hose around his arms.

Sudi pressed hard, pushing her full weight against his stomach.

In the murky light, his stare looked alien and filled with hatred. And then he surprised her. His face came down, mouth wide, and he tried to bite her nose. She pulled back, feeling his teeth scrape over her skin. She cried out, filled with rage, and elbowed him hard, driving the breath from him in a loud whoosh.

"I'll never be able to be a Descendant," Sudi whimpered, afraid that she might have wounded the real Scott. "I hate this."

"All right, we have him," Meri yelled.

Scott kicked and thrashed as Sudi rolled up his shirt, and then Meri handed Dalila the lipstick from her pocket, and Dalila drew the eye of light on Scott's stomach. He heaved and hissed. Apparently, the symbol caused him pain.

Then Dalila stepped back and began to read.

"Hail to thee, Ra, king of the eastern sky in thy rising, even to thee who is called Atum at thy dawning. Yea, great Ra who comes as Khephera, the everlasting."

Dalila droned on, but Sudi stopped listening. Scott had pulled one hand free and was angrily shredding the panty hose.

Sudi nudged Dalila. "Can we get on with it?"

"We don't need a filibuster," Meri agreed. "Just recite the spell."

Dalila looked up and gasped. Scott had almost broken free.

"Force of the stars, we offer these words," Dalila continued shakily, pointing to the hieroglyphs, and then Meri and Dalila joined in. *"Pierce Scott's heart, and dispel the darkness. Tear the demon from his soul."*

They stepped back quickly and watched.

Nothing happened.

"Should we try again?" Sudi asked.

Then, slowly, a shadow leaked from the eye drawn on Scott's chest. The black mist rose, spiraling up; it curled around the branches overhead. Then it dropped to the ground and thickened into a bent-over creature, taller than a man, eight feet or more in height, with large, thick arms. Eyes formed, and the creature screamed. Its fury filled the air with an electrical charge.

"I don't think we did it right," Sudi said, taking another step back, pulling Dalila and Meri with her.

"Maybe we forgot something," Dalila said. She unrolled the papyrus again. When she looked up, her face was pale. "We should have drawn a protective ring around us before starting the incantation."

The demon fixed its attention on Sudi, its eyes strangely alluring. She stared back, fascinated.

"I think it just wants me," Sudi said, easing away from her friends; she wanted to make sure they wouldn't be harmed.

The silhouette streaked toward her, losing form, and swirled around her. She tried to control her fear and to think, but before she could consider a plan, the shadow engulfed her. The demon's hatred pulsed through her. Its poisonous vapor seeped into her mouth. The taste made her gag.

The pressure became unbearable. She collapsed to her knees and fell forward onto the cold mud, her nose pressed against moldering leaves. She tried to draw a breath, but the effort seemed too great. The pace of her heartbeat slowed. She was vaguely aware of Dalila and Meri calling to her, and then their voices grew too faint to hear.

She was dying, but even as her body wanted to let go and be released from the pain, her soul fought to hang on to life. Then she remembered the words that the woman had spoken to her inside the museum. She mumbled them now: "Re-Atum emerged from the primeval ocean and took the form of a Bennu-bird. Then he flew from the darkness and perched on a rock. When he opened his beak, his cry broke the silence, and he created what is and what is not to be."

Maybe she would have more strength as the Bennu-bird. She tried to transform, but she felt too weak.

She concentrated, and this time feathers fluttered around her, and she changed into the bird. She opened her beak. "I speak these terrible words of power; send the demon hovering over me back to the chaos where he belongs."

The words came out as a primal scream that shattered the night and echoed around her.

Immediately, the pressure lifted and Sudi was transformed back into a girl.

The shadow wavered about her.

Sudi watched the black fog pull itself into a silhouette again. The demon opened his mouth, weeping loudly, and looked at her as if repenting for the crimes he had been forced to commit for the lord of chaos.

"He doesn't want to go back," Dalila said, joining Sudi.

"I know," Sudi answered. She pitied the demon, an emotion she had not expected to feel, and suddenly she wished she had spoken other words. Maybe she could have released him from his enslavement to Seth. She understood the reason the woman had used the word "terrible" to describe the words of power.

Then the demon vanished, leaving only its stench and a withering vapor.

"What did you do?" Meri asked.

As Sudi told her friends, she felt both elated and frightened, but mostly sad that she hadn't been able to save the creature.

"The Bennu's cry is the primal scream of creation," Dalila said. "You have the power to change what is."

Sudi shook her head. "I don't think it was

me," she whispered, "but another force. A greater power came through me."

They stared at each other, and then Sudi gazed up at the stars and prayed to the universe to guide her and help her speak the words of power more wisely.

"I think we've been successful," Dalila said.

"Except for the fact that we still have a love god running lose on Capitol Hill," Meri said with a huge grin.

"Hey!" a voice yelled.

"We forgot about Scott," Meri squealed.

Sudi was already running back to him. He looked bad: bewildered and covered with bruises.

He held up the shredded panty hose, then dropped them. "What did you do to me?" he asked, touching his swelling nose.

"I never did anything to you," Sudi said. She hadn't meant to hurt Scott, only the demon. "It's not what you think."

"I don't even know what I think," Scott said, and started to pull down his shirt. He traced his finger over the lipstick markings on his chest. "What's this eye for?"

Sudi couldn't even think of a lie to explain what they had done to him. She looked to Meri, hoping she could come up with an explanation. Meri shook her head and turned to Dalila, who shrugged.

"Something important," Sudi mumbled.

Scott glanced down at the dried blood embedded in his fingernails, then at the scratches on Sudi's arm. "Do I need to apologize for something?"

"It wasn't you," Sudi said.

"Then what was it?" Scott asked. "You look like someone dragged you through sand and mud."

Sudi shrugged. She knew how she must appear to him. She had seen herself in the mirror at the spa.

"I really like you, Sudi," Scott said. "But I don't know, you do some weird stuff." He shook his head, and, without explaining more, he hobbled away.

Sudi started after him, then stopped as an unnatural breeze curled around her. "Oh, no," she whispered and looked at Dalila and Meri. "Is the demon back?"

Dalila and Meri stared back at her, unsure. The air thickened, then began to spin, glimmering with flashes of gold. Huge wings formed and encircled Sudi. She turned as the downy wreath of feathers was transformed into a woman's arms.

Meri breathed out in a whistle and Dalila's eyes widened with awe.

"I am Isis," the woman said, "she of many names and daughter of Nut. I hold the greatest secrets of the universe, and I give my magic to the three of you."

Three rings appeared, hovering in the air. The sacred eye of Horus was fashioned in the gold with lapis lazuli and green faience.

"Seth caused the loss of the eye," Isis spoke softly. "But I restored it. The symbol is most powerful."

She slipped the first ring on Dalila's finger. "The ring of Isis bestows my favor and protection."

Then she guided the second onto Meri's hand. "All who see it will know you are my sisters."

At last Isis faced Sudi. "You especially have proven yourself strong," Isis said as she placed the last ring on Sudi's finger. "You were called to a life you didn't want, and you have accepted what fate has given to you."

Then Isis started to disappear, her body wavering in the breeze.

"Wait," Sudi said. "I have a thousand questions."

"Many blessings, my sisters," the goddess said, and then she vanished.

The girls stood in stunned silence, staring at their rings.

"Well," Meri whispered, smiling with happiness and triumph.

Dalila seemed pleased; she kept turning her hand to make the stones reflect the street light.

"And now we're sisters," Sudi said with a burst of emotion.

"Sisters!" Dalila and Meri shouted. They caught Sudi and and hugged her, kissing her cheeks until Sudi was laughing and pushing them away.

"I'll see you tomorrow," Sudi said, grateful that she would.

After leaving her friends, Sudi spoke the incantation for transforming into a bird. This time she focused her attention on her arms.

Feathers grew from her fingers, hands, and skin, fanning into wings. She ran down the street, until the wind caught her and lifted her above the trees. She soared, half girl, half bird, pure goddess, toward the rising moon, enjoying the enchantment of this night. They had been victorious, but she knew that this was only the first of many battles.

DON'T MISS THE NEXT
SISTERS OF ISIS BOOK,

Divine One

The storm was worse than any Meri had seen since she and her mother had moved into the old Victorian house in Washington, D.C. Lightning blazed across the night, and within three seconds, thunder exploded. A short burst of hail hammered the windows, then stopped, leaving only the patter of rain on the glass. Meri couldn't rid herself of the strange and frightening feeling that the storm was somehow directed at her, a prophetic sign of bad days ahead.

A sharp hiss made her look down as lightning flashed again, illuminating her bedroom with shuddering light. A dark form crept across the carpet, tail flexing back and forth.

"Don't be afraid, Miwsher," she said as thunder rattled the walls. She assumed that the storm had frightened her normally bold cat.

She tossed back her covers and jumped out of bed, but as she started to run after Miwsher, her foot landed in something wet. She paused and swept her toes across a soggy groove in the carpet, then looked up, expecting to see rain trickling from the ceiling; after all, the house had been built in 1840. She didn't see a leak, but she did see her cat, perched on top of the tall chest of drawers.

Meri spun around. If Miwsher was there, then what was the other creature?

The backyard bordered on Rock Creek Park, and although bears no longer roamed in the wilderness behind their house, raccoons and foxes did. Maybe a small animal had used Miwsher's cat door to come inside and escape the downpour.

Meri tiptoed after the fleeing shadow, imagining the poor stray shivering with fear, but at the same time she didn't follow too closely, in case the trespasser was a skunk.

As she neared the stairs, an unfamiliar, musty odor filled the gloom. The scent reminded her of cucumbers and wet soil, and although not bad, some deep instinctual pulse within her took over. She stepped more cautiously now, and didn't understand her fear.

The middle landing formed a balcony from which she could see down into the living room below. As she leaned over the banister, wind hit the tall windows behind her, and the sudden noise made her jump. Thin branches slapped the panes. The leafless twigs made odd ticking sounds, louder than the rain.

She eased down the remaining steps, clutching the handrail so tightly her fingers ached. When she reached the bottom of the staircase, a metallic crash came from her mother's home office, startling her.

It wasn't unusual for her mother to work late. She was the senior senator from California and had made one run for her party's presidential nomination. Next election everyone said she'd succeed. That worried the opposition party, but it also worried Meri.

The last time her mother had been a candidate, Secret Service agents had gone everywhere with Meri, including the high school dances. Their constant chaperoning had inhibited her. She was fifteen and still hadn't kissed a guy; not even a tight-lipped peck like most girls got on a dare in sixth grade. How pathetic was that? Some of her friends back home were seriously discussing birth control. She could only imagine how unexciting her love life would be if her mother actually won the election.

Then a bigger worry took over. Eventually, the agents would discover Meri's secret, and as sworn law-enforcement officers, what would they do? Was magic against the law?

She already feared that photographers would take her picture when she was doing something freakish. Her mother had hired two bodyguards to protect Meri from the paparazzi, but after Meri had learned about her true identity, Meri knew she couldn't expose the two men to the dangers she had to face. It had been hard enough convincing her mother that she didn't need the two-man escort. She couldn't picture trying to convince the Treasury Department that the protection of the Secret Service wasn't necessary.

Meri paused in the doorway to her mother's office expecting to see the four-footed intruder padding across the desk. The night-light cast a pallid glow over the bookshelves, but nothing looked disturbed. Meri entered the room, brushing her hand across the polished wood, then gazed out the window and surveyed the backyard. Wind had toppled the iron lawn furniture and pushed it against the stones in the rock garden. Maybe that explained the sound she had heard.

From the corner of her eye, she caught a shadow moving toward her. She whipped around and bumped into someone. Before she could scream, a hand covered her mouth, and she breathed in the almond fragrance of her mother's hand lotion.

"It's me." Her mother spoke into Meri's ear.

"Mom," Meri said, her heart still pounding from the impact. She started to flip on the overhead lights, but her mother stopped her.

"Someone's in the house," her mother whispered.

"It's only a stray, or maybe a skunk," Meri said. "I forgot to lock Miwsher's cat door."

"No animal could make the noise I'm talking about," her mother said. "I heard the side gate opening."

Twice when they were living in California someone had bypassed the alarm system and broken into their home. Now Meri wondered why her mother was prowling around the house like a detective, instead of calling the police.

Before Meri could ask, lightning struck the oak tree in the backyard, splitting the trunk. The night glowed orange, pulsing with spectral brightness, before fading back to gloom. Thunder shook the house. The vibration rumbled up Meri's legs and through her body.

Outside, sparks sputtered and swarmed around the branches, igniting twigs. Small fires spat more embers into the wind as rain quenched the flames. After that, the security lights went out. Immediately, the alarm system began bleeping, signaling that it had switched to battery power. Then the sound died.

For the second time that night, Meri had an eerie sense of foreboding that the storm's fury was directed at her.